LIKE A SISTER

LIKE A SISTER

A NOVEL

Janice
Daugharty

HarperCollins*Publishers*

FIRST EDITION

Designed by Kyoko Watanabe

Library of Congress Cataloging-in-Publication Data

Daugharty, Janice, 1944–
    Like a sister : a novel / Janice Daugharty. — 1st ed.
      p. cm.
    ISBN 0-06-019360-3
    I. Title
    PS3554.A844 L54 1999
    813'.54—dc21   99-15621

99 00 01 02 03 ❖/RRD 10 9 8 7 6 5 4 3 2 1

For my mother and sisters at the heart of this story.
And of course for Larry.

LIKE A SISTER

PART 1

1956

*S*ISTER IS THIRTEEN AND OLD-
est in the family, old enough to recall the peace of crickets
singing, young enough to believe that peace is still possible. Till she has to quit caring.

What Sister hears now are her brat brothers fighting
and her baby sister squealing and the neighbors saying . . .
The baby is Sister's, from her mother, Marnie, to lug on her
hip up and down the lane and along the highway leading
into Cornerville. To hear what she doesn't even know she
is hearing till she gets up some size and the neighbors start
saying—in looks that tell—how that trashy bunch of
Odumses have opened the old café and invaded the neighborhood.

Sister cannot say exactly when or where she was when
she first saw—heard—that look, and maybe it was some-
time at night after she lay down to sleep, but she saw it.
Then her eyes sprang wide and her lips parted and she
repeated over and over like a sinner's prayer how she
would not sorry away like Marnie, whose fixed-up face

loomed in a nimbus like the face of Jesus in the picture at church, even as Sister tried to despise her.

But Sister doesn't know how yet, or even what it is that she will do or not do, what it is that she's seen—heard—on the faces of the neighbors. Or even that she will have to figure it all out before she can do or not do *it*. She marvels, thinking back, at how she has sallied off to school, Before Knowledge, feeling her hair in class. Everybody but her knowing that you don't sit and pinch the ends of your hair in public, or pick your nose, or scratch the ringworm on your butt.

Her face burns recalling all the careless things she's done—just functioning, doing what feels good. That ease of living, stuffed but starving, feeling good. She thinks about the feel-good tricks she taught Sueann Horton in her backyard at the Sampson Camp, north of Cornerville, and about Sueann's mother sending Sister home in shame.

She makes herself miserable with remembering and watching to see who sees what she isn't yet sure is the right or the wrong things to do, to be. When she goes to Sade's Café, to visit Marnie, she has to be on the lookout for neighbors watering their flowers or sitting on their porches.

"Shh!" she says to the baby and blows at gnat drifts in the guttering sunlight. Listening out to hear if they are talking about the threat of rain, the Russians, or the Odumses. Suddenly Sister notices that the baby is filthy—tarry patches of chewed bubble gum on her pale face and chest. The bird-boned baby with sheer white hair grins and grabs Sister's nose and rises high in Sister's arms so that she has to wag her head from side to side to see the barefoot-tracked path to the café. When Sister holds the baby up to the sun, she can almost see through her. A miracle of rubbery flesh, blue veins, and pink bones.

Glitter in the sand, like the glitzy red and blue fenders of the café jukebox, and that "Mister Sandman" song that makes Sister long for the old days of early spring, when she would get so happy that the nerves in her kneecaps would jump. Smoke from cigarettes, french fries, and burned hamburger grease. She has been served fried chicken before, right here. Once.

She locks her knees and hoists the baby higher. Wet diaper chapping Sister's arm like salt rubbed into her mosquito bites. She sits at one of the close round tables and bounces the baby on her lap. She can see the faces of two teenage boys seated at the bar in the gold-flecked mirror on the wall ahead. Can see her own bronzy cast against the baby's bluish pallor. Sister's hair is black and straight, with bangs. Chinese eyes and full lips that don't figure. The two boys, one black-headed with a chubby heart face and the other blond and angular, are snickering into glasses of Cherry Coke.

Marnie's latest man, Sade Odums, stands in the kitchen doorway with his thumbs hooked in his tooled leather belt. A blond giant with more scalp than hair and hard blue eyes that pinch his face into a mad stare.

"Where's Marnie?" Sister asks, too loud now that the song on the jukebox has quit; the automatic arm judders the record back to its slot. A low hum.

"In the back room," says Sade. "Be out in a jiff."

The boys mock strangle, giggle.

"Y'all behave yourself now," Sade says to the boys and starts toward Sister. "Whatcha want, Sister?" he asks.

"The twins is cussing and carrying on something awful. Keep messing up the kitchen evertime I clean it up." Same thing she said last time—any excuse to keep a check on Marnie. To get close again. Before Sade, between the other boyfriends and husbands, Sister and Marnie were close. She misses Marnie. Misses combing her soft brown hair, misses painting her flat nails, misses scratching her pimply back.

"Tell 'em I said to settle down." Sade hard-eyes the boys at the bar, whose white teeth flash in the mirror.

Long-bodied and tall with hiked shoulders, the blond boy gets up and fishes in his pants pocket, then crosses the square room to the jukebox.

"Say, Sade," calls the other boy, "whatcha charge for just watching?"

The boy at the jukebox laughs, drops his nickel in the slot.

The sun, dropping likewise, beyond the plate-glass windows, shows grease smears and handprints and "Sade's Café" spelled backwards. Sister studies the words and tries to make them mean something new. The baby reaches for a ketchup bottle in the middle of the table and knocks it over. It rolls to the dirty white tiles and keeps rolling till it gets to a corner where a dead cockroach lies on its back with its hairy legs raised to glory.

"Awright," says Sade to the boys. "One of y'all go on in, but hold it down back there. I got younguns here."

The boy at the bar slides from his stool and swaggers through the greasy white curtain partition to the kitchen, meeting another boy coming out.

"Oh, man!" says the boy at the jukebox and adjusts his narrow silver belt.

Sister watches the new boy join him, both skinny in blue dungarees and brown loafers—Mister Sandman, bring me a dream.

"Take the baby and go on to the house," says Sade to Sister, motioning to the door. "Marnie's seeing to customers."

And then Sister knows how the old café, which everybody has said wouldn't stay open two months, has stayed open from March to May. Knows what she's been seeing—hearing—from the neighbors.

*O*N SUNDAYS SISTER GOES TO the Baptist church, north side of the café, same as she goes to traveling tent shows in summer on the vacant lot south side of the café. Same as she goes to school functions in fall and winter, at the old brick schoolhouse in the southeast section of Cornerville, a town she pictures as quartered by the crossing of Highways 129 and 94. Any store that is open, Mondays through Saturdays, Sister goes into. She goes to the post office across from the courthouse; she goes to the library *inside* the courthouse. Something to do, now doing out of habit and with the needling need to rise above. She and the baby and the boys in Sunday school, then church: silent, white, and holy. Concrete blocks that Sister can count while the preacher preaches, while she itches but doesn't scratch, and if her nose clogs till she passes out from lack of air, she won't pick it. Won't let the baby, perched on her lap, suck her thumb, finger her ears, or whine.

Sister always takes along a bottle for the baby and now

stoppers her mouth with the nipple when it opens. The baby sprawls in Sister's arms and squeezes her eyes shut, sucking. Her pink dress rides up at the yoke to the dirt necklace on her neck. Though Sister and the twins are known in Cornerville as Odumses, the baby is Marnie's only child by Sade; Sister has had maybe a half dozen last names over the years, her brothers almost as many, because Marnie signs them up for school with the last name of the man she is with at the time, married or not.

Because Sister's eyes and ears have been newly opened, she is aware of everybody squirming around to eye her and the baby—neither of them making a peep, for once!—Dot Knight, her Sunday school teacher, among them.

"Y'all might not want to stay for church," she'd said after Sunday school that morning. "Y'all" being Sister, who would carry the message to her brothers, the twins, in another class.

"We're staying," Sister had said. She would show everybody how she had changed, how Marnie had changed—even if she hadn't changed.

"Suit yourself," Dot said, "but we got a business meeting after preaching, and I wouldn't stay for that if I was you."

Sister is weary of moving from place to place: The last was Quitman, Georgia, where Marnie had to sneak out of town in the middle of the night, dodging wives and debts. At least when Marnie and Sister had lived in Blountstown, near the Florida Gulf, with Sister's real daddy, they'd known peace. From there, onward and eastward, Marnie has left a trail of lusting men and short handed employers. One day she'll meet a rich man, she says, and she will be dripping in diamonds and furs.

Sister likes to imagine herself as Baby Athena Kaye in a lacy white cap, in a ruffle-skirted bassinet, left to sun in the Blountstown backyard, where crickets sing in the grass. She imagines a parade of faces—the same two faces, her mama and her daddy, over and over—smiling down at Athena Kaye smiling up. But then when she lets the truth in, she is older, two or so, and her daddy is at work and she is standing in a porch swing next to Marnie with that look of leaving even then, had Sister been smart enough to recognize it, and all that's left of her imagined picture is the sound of crickets singing in the grass.

The baby on Sister's lap passes from shallow to deep sleep, see-through lids twitching, then going still as a doll's when laid flat on its back. Sister wiggles the nipple from her pink lips, leaving a pearl of milk that rolls across the baby's sucked right cheek to the oily cotton in her ear—earache. Yesterday, Sister had taken the baby to her neighbor Mrs. Willington, who had doctored her ear with neat's-foot oil and ordered Sister to keep her out of the night air and not let her mess with the cotton. Not that easy. Sister keeps finding the cotton wad in the baby's mouth, in her crib, and lives in dread of the yellow-haired old lady finding out and refusing to doctor the baby next time she gets croup.

Sister can feel her own lids closing and a sweet numbing start in her face, her fingers, her toes. The preacher drones on with the ceiling fan, words thinning out in Sister's ears. She loves dozing in church—cool in the mist of white light and aroma of book mold, safe from the devil's grip for a couple of hours a week. She has been saved in every town she's lived in and is thinking about getting saved again. As soon as they start singing "Just as I Am" after preaching.

Suddenly she sits up, listening to a thumping sound on the roof that turns to sliding. The preacher stops, listening too, then goes on preaching while the thumping travels end to end of the church roof.

One of the deacons, Ray Williams, two pews ahead of Sister, gets up and tiptoes along the center aisle and out the door at her back. A newcomer to Cornerville but a town big shot, Williams is to Sister as Santa Claus is to children—some fake you pretend to like till after Christmas. Twice he has asked Sister to leave church with the squealing baby.

The racket on the roof stops and starts, and each time the thumping commences, everybody starts whispering and the preacher lifts his eyes heavenward but keeps on preaching about lost lambs. One coming back to the fold.

The church door opens and closes again with a shuffle and click, and in a few seconds somebody taps Sister on the shoulder. She turns around, and Ray Williams's tapered tan face is so close she can see herself in his green-tinted clip-on sunshades.

"Come on out here," he whispers.

Sister gathers the limp baby in her arms, picks up the

bottle and her Sunday school book, and follows him out-side.

The sun hurts her eyes as she backs across the dirt road that leads alongside the café to the church and peers up at the twins climbing toward the pitch of the green roof. Mickey spies Sister and yells at Paul and they push higher, faster, with their bare toes and vanish over the peak where puffy white clouds scud in the blue sky.

"I tried to talk 'em down," says Ray Williams, grinning with his hands in his black serge pants pockets. He wears a ring with lots of keys jangling from a belt loop. His wavy brown hair is combed straight back from his high forehead.

"Hey, Paul, Mickey!" yells Sister. "Y'all get down from there right now or I'm telling." Eyes on the roof, she wan-ders around the left front corner of the church, baby on her shoulder like a bundle of dough. Just as she gets to the northeast wing, she sees them squirrel down the trunk of a live oak and strike out between the parked cars in the side yard of the church.

She doesn't realize that Ray Williams has followed her till she backs into him, his columnar body that looks lean but feels fat. He holds her shoulders, chuckling, till she yanks away. He crosses his arms over his blue-striped white shirt, speaking low and secretive: "Bet you old Sade'll take his belt to them for that, huh?"

"Would if I told," says Sister, shifting the baby to her other shoulder.

"But you ain't no tattletale, are you, Sister?"

She doesn't like his peppery cologne, she doesn't like his tone; she cannot see his eyes, only her own eyes in his clip-on sunshades, and those bubblegum-pink lips she probably wouldn't notice if she could see his eyes instead of her own. She steps to one side to withdraw her eyes from that face she doesn't like.

"Café business is doing good, I guess?" He gazes at the small, aqua-painted, concrete-block building, his horseshoe teeth shining yellow as the sun.

"Yessir," she says, watching houseflies buzz in the shimmery heat around the spillover of garbage cans at the café's rear door.

"That Sade's one smart businessman, I say," says Ray Williams. "Course ain't everybody'll agree with me." He nods toward the church where a song of Jesus leaks through the open jalousies—"Just as I Am."

Sister wants to go. She starts to go. But he's still talking, he's a grownup, he holds the key to the church door. She stops.

"Yes sir," he says, "a man's gotta do what he's gotta do. Sure beats hauling fence posts."

A wrap-up, Sister figures. "Well, I'll be seeing you, Mr. Ray."

"Ain't put you to work yet, has he?" He is now rocking on the elevated heels of his black wing tips.

"Nosir, not yet."

"You'd do good waiting on tables, quick and all, I bet."

The baby comes awake like a lily opening, grins, and

stretches back, so that Sister almost drops her. The waist of her pink dress hikes to her chin. Clabbered milk and pee claim the sagey smell of cured grass.

"Cute as a button," says Ray Williams, shifting foot to foot.

Sister thinks at first that he is talking about the baby, then sees that he is looking straight at her.

"Tell ol' Sade he won't see my name on no petition, not this fellow. And give him one of these for me." He plucks a small white card from his shirt pocket and hands it to her. "Running for county commission, tell him."

On her way to Baptist Training Union that evening, Sister almost crosses paths with The Judge on his way to the Methodist church. Halfway up the lane, she sees him step and poke with his cane, step and poke with his cane, from the vine-smothered red house and across the ell of grassed yard on the left corner of Sister's lane. She slows walking, watching him amble on along the road shoulder leading into town. He is old, maybe older than anybody in Cornerville, Sister thinks, but his hair is wet black. He has on a white shirt and black pants, same as always, is narrow at the top and broad at the bottom, and the slowest man Sister has ever seen. Sometimes the twins will see him leaving his house, en route to church on Sunday mornings and evenings, and to the courthouse every other morning of the week, and they speed-walk up the lane, scooting their feet, get right up to him and cut, spinning dirt and making motor noises with their mouths. But that's not why Sister and the twins no longer go over to The Judge's big old house with the flower-garden yard and vanilla-warm kitchen and the fanciest outhouse in all of Swanoochee County (Sister is something of an expert on outhouses). They no longer go because last summer Marnie claimed The Judge was judging her because every time he saw her, he would say, "Lord in heaven help!" Same as always, what he always says, like a prayer. Sister and the twins hated giving up Mrs. Judge's home cooking and playing with the grandkids visiting from Florida, but Marnie had dared them to step foot inside either the house or the yard again. (Sister still sneaks over to use The Judge's pull-chain facility with a crescent moon sawed out of the vertical board door and a winding path lined with magenta periwinkles and cherry-tomato bushes, when she cannot get up the courage to go inside the dim, snaky, fecal-reeking toilet behind her own house.)

But more than Mrs. Judge's pound cake, warm under its aluminum cover on the long dining table; more than the outhouse and the slow, settled ways of the old pair, and those grandchildren all the way from South Florida, Sister misses the parade of eager young lovers coming to The Judge to get married: no waiting period for blood tests in Swanoochee County, no parental-consent forms or witnesses in tow behind the JUST MARRIED car. Though usually at a moment's notice, The Judge can summon a witness from the neighborhood. Sister herself has been called on a number of times to go get Willa from the Lamar house across the highway.

Once, when Willa couldn't come because her youngest daughter, Pat, had measles, a couple from Somewhere, Tennessee, got married in front of the Lamars' living room mantelpiece, and Sister had watched it all. Sister watched them kiss.

The Judge has passed through the shady stretch between the lane and the café and is moseying along the sunny blacktop in front of the courtyard, when Sister starts to turn off to the Baptist church. Suddenly she spies a white sheet of paper tacked to the café door. She walks up to the jalousied door that mirrors her body in disconnected bands and reads the typed print on the paper: "This is an official petition from the members of Cornerville Baptist Church to Sade's Café, duly stating that we object to the sin associated with your place of business." Then a list of names, Dot Knight's among them, but not Ray Williams's, just Mrs. Ray's. Sister feels sure that he is trying to play both sides to get more votes and therefore get elected county commissioner. She has not given his card to Sade, who sleeps all day on Sunday, he and Marnie, and won't give it to him now. And she won't go back to the Baptist church, even if the blind gospel group comes to sing every Sunday night. Though she hates to deprive herself of that, almost feels that her pride isn't worth such a sacrifice.

She rips down the sheet of paper, folds it, and puts it in the pocket of her blue-and-brown striped dress with its gathered skirt and deep hem that collects sand—a mystery. Then she walks fast, past the Baptist church, where children are calling out to one another as they dodge among the parked cars, till she gets to the courtyard with its white pipe railing.

On Sundays Cornerville is almost empty, as if even the traffic passing through on the way to Florida has been rerouted. A cold closed feeling of being alone in the world till Monday, when Mr. King's filling station at the crossing of Highways 129 and 94 will be clotted with idle old men and pulpwood trucks, and the dingy white two-story courthouse will suck in and send out the lazy tide of lawmakers and lawbreakers. The two-story, red-brick Masonic building, south of Mr. King's, leans in shadow across the gravel road, bright blue curtains covering the windows, but the door is ajar.

The only building along the brief business row in Cornerville that Sister has never stepped foot inside of and now the door is ajar. If she'd suddenly gone lame, she would have crawled across the highway to get there. Just for a peep inside—what do the Masons do in there?

She crosses the highway, looking both ways and all around.

Nobody. Nothing. Not even one of the dogs that generally roams the business stretch.

She pushes the door all the way open and steps into

the doorway of the dim, musty room. On her right is a standing stack of folded wooden chairs, and above, on the brick wall, hanging from hooks are several purple satin robes with gold trim. Peeping around the door, on her left she sees a long wooden church-type pew with parchment booklets on one end: key to what the Masons are about, what they do at monthly meetings. She will take one, but first the stairs along the back wall, leading up to the room with the strange blue curtains. But when she gets to the middle of the room, in the dense heat and mustiness, she hears low laughing and talking upstairs. She stops, listening, and can tell only that the voices belong to two men. If she were lame, she would crawl. One step, two steps, and she is on the bottom stair, easing up, voices louder but not clearer. Halfway there, holding her breath now, she hears a thump on the floor, stops and waits, more laughing, talking—forget the books, she is about to learn firsthand about the Masons. Word is at school that to become a Mason a new member has to first ride a goat.

Nearing the top step, she does crawl, expecting to see the two men the voices belong to right away, but instead finds herself alone in a dusty closetlike alcove paneled in pine that gives off a reddish glow like Sade's oxblood boot polish. No door into the room where the men and the goat or whatever are—just a matter of steps away. Still on her hands and knees, she crawls toward the doorway. Stops as she recognizes Ray Williams's voice: ". . . dollars to be had . . . Cuba . . . in on it." The other man mumbles.

A faint scratching sound, then the smell of sulfur, then cigarette smoke. No goat unless you count Ray Williams as one.

Outside, the Masonic building shadow has stretched across 129, up to the courtyard, and Sister has to hurry or be late for church. She follows the white pipe railing to the corner, facing Hoot Walters's white board store and the adjoining post office with its blue shake roof and gingerbread trim, fronting 94, then crosses the gravel road when she gets to the red-brick Methodist church. A white steeple pierces the fading blue sky.

She feels free and light without the baby, who has stayed with Marnie. She was just waking up, cross and scavenging for food, when Sister left for church, and Sister can't help longing for the Marnie—before Sade, between men—who would pile the children in the backseat of her 1951 blue-and-white Ford Victoria (where and how she got the car is another mystery). Marnie and Sister in the front, out for a Sunday evening ride: just riding—Marnie swigging beer and smoking and telling Sister about her boyfriends, what she had dreamed the night before. Sometimes Marnie would get low because her weight was up, and Sister would trim her hair on the front porch and then anchor her feet while she did sit-ups. "Don't let me eat," she'd say to Sister, "no matter what. Not till I get rid of this

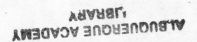

gut." Sister would starve with her. Not even a Zero candy bar for two or three days.

This evening Sister had to slip off from the twins, who will probably show up at the Baptist church again, as well as from Marnie, who was expecting Sister to cook. Marnie wouldn't understand the significance of getting respectable, would think Sister was going to church to get out of work. When Marnie and Sade had opened the café in March, Marnie had let Sister have the new blond bedroom suite she had bought on credit for herself as prepayment for Sister keeping the children and the house while Marnie worked. So far Sister hasn't been able to manage either, and Marnie is forever threatening to take the bedroom suite away. Sister doesn't care about the furniture, that spiteful reminder, but she does hate to let Marnie down. And for that reason, she hasn't told about the twins disrupting church that morning; also she fears that if she tells, Marnie might somehow twist their mischief into mischief done against them, against herself, and go to the Baptist church and start a fight (Marnie will fight for her children, Sister can say that much for her), and then Sade might get fired up and start preaching about all the busybody Christians in Cornerville. Not that Sade has anything against religion, he's quick to add, but that bunch of hypocrites . . .

Sister knows the spiel as well as the stories in the Bible, which she reads as fairy tales and whose characters she casts as select people in Cornerville, depending on her moods: Sometimes Solomon is Hoot Walters, sometimes

The Judge; Satan is Sade; The Prodigal Son is Mickey, who is ten. Her neighbor Willa Lamar is Jesus. Today Marnie is Mary Magdalene.

~~~

Methodists and Baptists are a lot alike, Sister decides, except that Methodists are prissier, sing proper, and their preachers are sent by the Methodist delegation instead of called by the Lord. She doesn't know many Methodists personally, meaning that in the old days, before she became respectable, she hadn't taken up at their houses. Except for The Judge, second pew on the left, who is now standing and outsinging the Sunday-night congregation on "What a Friend We Have in Jesus" in that same upturned scolding voice used on couples stopping by to get married—"Papers, please." Sister knows Sueann and her mother, of course—the mama who sent her home for playing nasty with her daughter. But Mrs. Horton is now Sunday-friendly to Sister, except when Sueann tries to sit with her. Then Mrs. Horton motions Sueann to the choir, and when the choir gets through singing and files from the loft to take their regular seats for preaching, the round smiley woman keeps a hand on Sueann's head to steer her to the slick pine pew across the aisle from Sister.

While the preacher preaches—a milder form of the Baptist sermon that morning—Sister takes the petition from her pocket and reads the names. Some she knows, most she doesn't. All fit into the faces of the multitudes that Jesus fed fish. Or the crowd in the temple with the money changers, whom Jesus scattered. No, *Samson and Delilah*—the movie Sade took them to see at the drive-in theater in Jasper, Florida, across the state line. The crowd of Philistines gathered around the courthouse-or-whatever when Samson shook the pillar loose and toppled the whole building on their heads.

In Sister's mind picture, Marnie is Delilah.

In two weeks' time, posters with Ray Williams's you-can-count-on-me face begin cropping up on power poles and tree trunks: VOTE FOR RAYFORD WILLIAMS, COUNTY COMMIS-SIONER. HE'LL DO YOU A GOOD JOB.

Suddenly he is everywhere. A swastika on the walls of the courthouse, the post office, Sirman's and King's filling stations. All except the grocery store of Williams's opponent, Hoot Walters.

On the way to and from school, on Monday, Sister stomachs Ray Williams's face, which now represents everybody in the town out to damn Marnie. But after school on Tuesday, brain dulled by behaving seven straight hours in a row, she begins pondering workable paybacks. Her body tingles with anticipation.

She is supposed to go straight to Willa Lamar's after school to pick up the bab, but decides instead to go home first. She has to pass right by the white frame house across 129 to get to the dirt lane leading to her own house. The baby is in her playpen on the Lamars' porch, and when she sees Sister, she holds to the wood slats, stands, and squeals, but Sister walks on toward the longish brown house side-set at the end of the lane on a background of green woods. The shady yard is littered with empty Kool-Aid and cola bottles, paper trash, rain-filled tires, and Sade's junk cars. No grass or flowers like the yards of other houses at the start of the lane, like the Lamars' kaleidoscopic yard across the highway. Just brown leaves and dirt that generate a perpetual dingy light, spring, summer, fall, and winter, as if viewed through brown whiskey-bottle glass.

Inside she goes straight to her dim bedroom with the bright blond bedroom suite to wait till the twins clear out of the kitchen at the rear of the house. As soon as they figure there is no food in the house, they will go to Mr. Sirman's station, south of the café, where they will charge candy, Popsicles, bubble gum, and drinks to Sade. Another problem that makes Sister want to pinch her hair and pick her nose: When Sade finds out how much she and the twins have been charging, he is going to raise hell.

After the twins have slammed out the back door, Sister goes to the kitchen and rummages through a cabinet drawer of bent spatulas, rusty knives, and crumpled receipts till she finds a black freezer-paper marker. Then she slips it into her blue skirt pocket and sets out up the lane to the house across the highway. Again, when the baby spies Sister from the Lamars' front porch, she stands in her playpen, holding on to one side, and squeals.

Sister walks up on the porch, with its white slat swing and hanging birdcage, home to the blue-green parakeet, Zelda. Hands each side of her face and peeping through the screen door she calls, "Willa?"

"Yoo-hoo," Willa calls back from the kitchen at the rear of the house.

"I'm here for the baby."

"Okay. Just see she doesn't get dirty before night; I gave her a bath a while ago."

Sister lifts the baby from the playpen and sits her straddled one hip. She smells of baby powder, feels smooth but light and breakable as a hollow chocolate bunny. Sister shortcuts across the grassy lot between the Lamars' doll-like house and Miss Willington's aged-gray farmhouse to the path under the live oaks along the west side of the highway.

The dumpy old lady is crouched in one of the calico-aproned rockers on her front porch, hieing a fly flappet and watching the café.

Sister checks the baby's waxy right ear for the wad of cotton—gone. "How you, Miss Willington?" she says.

"Keep that baby in out of the damp now, you hear?" says Mrs. Willington.

Next time Sister gets ground itch, she will suffer and savor sawing the edge of the bed sheet between her toes till they are bloody raw, but she will not go back to Miss

Willington and hold her feet up over a smoldering pine branch to get cured.

The first Ray Williams poster, on the way into Cornerville, is tacked to one of the mammoth live-oak trunks before Miss Willington's picket gate. Directly above it is a picture poster of President Eisenhower, bland-faced as a baby. Of course, with Miss Willington on the porch, Sister can't do much about the Williams poster right now. But, stopping to shift the baby to her other hip, Sister studies the poster for how to redesign it.

She keeps walking, keeping to the left side of the highway to avoid the twins at Mr. Sirman's filling station, a one-room wooden building set behind red double gas pumps on a concrete island in the gray dirt.

All evening Sister dodges the neighbors while she locates and redesigns posters, traipsing over all four quarters of Cornerville from the dividing line of the main crossing. A couple of times she gets so high on her art that she almost forgets she is now respectable and almost—*almost*—does it in front of people wandering from Hoot Walters's store to the post office, to the courthouse.

Tired and hungry, she walks home in the dusk spiced with supper smells: frying bacon, browning biscuits, and sweet, steeped tea. One more poster to go—the oak in front of Miss Willington's house. Sister has made it past the café with its blaring jukebox without giving in to the urge to see Marnie, and is again under the row of live oaks. Miss Willington is not on the porch this time, and a yellow light shines from the back along the open hall. But if she were on the porch, Sister thinks she might do it anyway, risking all just to complete the job.

She sets the baby on the dirt, spanks her hands for eating acorns, and faces the sign that says, VOTE FOR RAYFORD WILLIAMS, COUNTY COMMISSIONER. HE'LL DO YOU A GOOD JOB.

Starting on the bottom line, she crosses out "a good job" and writes on the top line "donot"—one word as in "cannot"—and begins worrying that all along she's been writing "donot," or maybe "donut," instead of "do not." Though she has nothing against this Eisenhower fellow— the president—she reaches up high and touches up his faded eyebrows and hair. Draws him some lips. PEACE AND PROSPERITY, says the slogan. He looks evil, like the devil, or like a poster touched up by a communist kid with a black freezer marker. She looks back to see if The Judge is on his porch, looks down and the baby is gone.

With fear like bubble gum stuck in her throat, she searches around the four oaks, scans up and down the darkening highway, the yards of two lit white houses across the road, and finally heads out for Willa's house to get help. Crossing the lot in the level dusk, between the Lamars' and Miss Willington's, she spots the baby crawling through the tall grass toward Willa, who is watering pink petunias along the north side of her house. Stocky and dark in a pink sundress, Willa has her back to the baby, green water hose trailing as she steps along the white wall, spraying flowers in the hiss and sing of a crystal arc.

The swirled-butter cat named Larry, who belongs to Willa's daughter Pat, is moving like slow pale water through the tall green grass.

Sister creeps toward the baby, now sitting to nibble something in her hand, hoping she can scoop her up before Willa turns around, but just as Sister gets to the corner of the yard, Willa fans the arc of water around and eyes the baby with a shocked look.

"What in the *world*?" she says, dropping the hose and darting toward her. And then to Sister, easing up, "What is this poor lil' ol' baby doing out here this time of evening? *What?*" She lifts the baby under her arms and hugs her, mumbling to herself. "I swannee! I don't know how your mama can leave a youngun with a youngun without no thought atall."

*O*N SATURDAY IT RAINS. A slow rain with birdsong in the misty green light of the lane to Sister's house—wet, brown, and dreary where the woods start. The rooty smell of rotting leaves and a lonesome tune of ticking in the black gums that separate the Odumses' yard from the Negro quarters in the east, where at times, if Sister listens, she can hear a mimicry of hoots and cries as if in echo of the Odums household.

While the baby naps Sister stands on her platform porch with its broken railing and pee-sopped diapers and watches Willa's three girls dancing in the May Day shower in their front yard. Used to, Sister would have left the baby and dashed over there to play in her panties. Not now; she can't now. One, she is having to be respectable; and two, she isn't sure how Willa Lamar will treat her after the incident with the baby escaping.

She watches the three blond girls a while longer, then steps out into the rain, smiling because it tickles. What can such feeling good hurt? Nobody can see her, tucked back in the black gums from the highway. Wet leaves stick to her bare feet like soggy cornflakes, while the rain ticks through the trees and taps on Sade's junk cars.

She wishes Marnie would come home and Sade would go—as in leave for good—but figures it would be the other way around. This is *his* house, and he has taken them all in and in his own way is good to them, though he does sock Marnie around. Better than Will Nobles, in Douglas, who had broken Marnie's nose for flirting with his hunting buddies. But if Sade would go, Marnie might not be in trouble with the churches and she might change back into her old fun-loving self and she and Sister might go to the Alapaha River, where Marnie could dive from the bridge while Sister sits on the sand and pries open mussels look-ing for pearls. She would make a necklace for Marnie with the pearls—if pearls can be found in oysters, surely they can be found in mussels. And then she wonders for maybe the millionth time why Marnie, who hates Georgia dirt and Florida sand and little-town thinking, keeps getting bogged down in the same area. But as much as Sister sometimes likes a fresh start herself—the possibility that things might be better *this* time—she also worries that Marnie will load up her car one morning and be gone for-ever, or take Sister and the baby and the twins and they will find themselves in the middle of the big city, in the middle of the night, with no food, no house, just another strange man who, like Sister, believes that pearls might be found in mussels.

Sister has danced her way along the sandy lane with clear dimpling puddles, drawn by the girls across the highway, by the fairyland white house with its mysterious second front door and carousel-colored petunias. Zelda the blue-green parakeet sways on her perch in the wire cage above the white porch swing, where Larry the Cat is snoozing.

The sun breaks through the film of clouds and bathes the girls in yellow light. A green smell, clean and sparkling. Scarves of Spanish moss draping from the oaks along the highway. The baked-sugar smell of cake or maybe cookies—Sister can take her pick. She can feel the tickle of rain sliding down her sides, her mouth furry with gladness. Smell her own hair and her blood warming the rain.

A semi truck roars along the highway, wheels singing in the steamy trails of water and spraying her face. A peppering of hot gravel on her shins. In the languishing mist she spies Willa on her front porch watching her, and starts to turn around.

"Sister," Willa calls, "go get the baby. Bring her here and I'll look out for her while you play with the girls. It's May Day!"

Still, like a dog that's been whipped, Sister hangs back from the Lamars' after her May Day fling. But from then on, when she picks up the baby after school, Willa feeds her cookies or popcorn in waxed-paper cones. She even sends collard greens with hunks of ham home with Sister for supper. (Sister feels guilty for throwing out the slick, bitter, leathery greens and eating canned SpaghettiOs instead.) Some mornings Alda, Neida, and Pat, Willa's doorstep girls, wait to walk with Sister to school. Usually Sister is late, so the girls will be gone. Soon Sister begins to get up earlier, feeding the baby and heading out so she can walk with the girls. None of them is in Sister's class at school—Alda is fourteen, Neida is twelve, and Pat is ten—so they are never tested on whether they would pal around with Sister away from home. She sees them sometimes during the day, at recess, but doesn't go near them. What if they don't speak?

School will be out in a couple of weeks; then she will never know. She might die before school starts again in September and be spared knowing. That's how important it is for them to like her, that's how careful she is not to find out.

On the way to school one morning, Neida stops before the Ray Williams poster on Miss Willington's oak and laughs. "Look at that," she says. "Who you reckon did that?"

Sister's face burns.

Alda stops to look too. "I don't know," she says, "but somebody's got a lot of gumption."

Sister glows. Yes, she has done it, she wants to say. Yes, it is she who has all that gumption. Look what the poster really says: DO NOT VOTE FOR RAYFORD WILLIAMS, COUNTY COMMISSIONER. HE'LL DO YOU.

～

Daydreaming at school: To the chirring of the fan, which feels like a heater and looks like a huge green calamitous metal box bracketed to the bead-board wall above the blackboard, Sister cools herself in her desk at the end of the window row with memories of that cold January when her world had frozen over—was it Quitman, or Pelham, or Boston?—and Marnie had neglected or forgotten or couldn't scrape up the money to pay the gas bill. Late evening and Marnie was lugging the bundled-up twins on her hips and Sister was trailing behind, dragging her mama's stuffed blue diaper bag like a toy on a string. Just out walking, it seemed like, in the slant of orange sun, in the windless cold, along a gravel road with side-by-side facing frame houses. Yet Sister knew that nothing was ever what it seemed like with Marnie—Marnie had on her good twead coat and Marnie had a plan. The twins were feverish, whining, croupy. All day, while Marnie was at work, the cold wind blew, and Sister had moved the twins with the sun—from front to side to back of the little rented house— trying to get them warm. When Marnie got home she had found them nestled against the old brick chimney of the boarded-up fireplace, and boy was she mad! She was mad at the gas man, mad at the man who rented her the house, mad at the twins' daddy, whom she had loved with all her heart only the day before and now hated with all her heart. Over, just like the wind.

At the end of the road, set back in a grove of pecan trees with stripped branches that touched the dusking sky, sat a white-painted brick building with yellow lights shining through small paned windows. There was a white sign out front with blocky black lettering. A fat man and a fat woman came out the door and started down the cobbled path. Books stacked in both their arms. The man had a kind round face and brown bangs like a boy's. He spoke to Marnie, but she didn't even speak. She stepped to one side of the brick path, twins hanging from her hips like saddlebags, her good tweed coat hiked above her knees.

Inside smelled of scorched dust and stamp-pad ink and was so warm it made Sister's face ache. Marnie stood the twins on the floor and held their hands, then walked them slow past the rest room doors and the water fountains and the two ashtrays on metal pedestals. They had sand in them. And on toward a long wooden counter with a green lamp on top and a short woman with dark curly hair behind it.

"We'll be closing in about fifteen minutes," she said to Marnie and picked up an armload of books and walked toward the north end of the open room—shelves of books from floor to the ceiling. Her shoe heels clicked on the wooden floor. She seemed tuned in to the rhythm of the clicking.

One of the twins sat down and started bawling and Marnie lifted him by an arm and set him astraddle her hip. The other twin was already toddling toward a low round table with small red chairs on the right. Books were scattered about on the table, on a brown wool rug before shelves of other books. Marnie sat in one of the little red chairs and held the crying baby in her arms till his eyes closed and his mouth opened, cheeks hot and red as the chair.

In a few minutes the curly-haired woman came back to the counter stationed centerwise the room. Sister could tell she was a fool about keeping things neat: She stamped the inside covers in back of a couple of books, slipped their cards from the pockets and stamped them too, then placed them in a narrow file with a zillion other cards and evened them all up with her hands. She snapped her stamp pad shut and pushed it to the very, very edge of the counter and placed the stamp with its little knob handle on top at the very, very edge of the stamp-pad tin. Done, she took a ring of keys from a drawer in the counter and started toward the entrance, jangling them meaningfully as she went from rest room to rest room switching off lights.

"Let's go," Marnie said and got up, cradling the sleeping child in her arms, and walked away.

Sister followed with the diaper bag and the other twin.

"Y'all come back on Monday," said the woman, meeting them at the water fountains. "Library hours are from ten in the morning till six in the evening, Mondays, Wednesdays, and Fridays."

"I can read," said Marnie and passed through the front door to the piney raw cold.

The sun had gone down, and there was a rim of lavender and a rim of rose where the curve of graying sky touched ground. The gaps between the silvery trunks of the pecan trees were almost filled in with dark. Just a slat of light from the door as Marnie peeped inside. "Shh," she said, though nobody was speaking or crying; no sound save for dogs barking somewhere and a train whistle thin and distant.

Suddenly Marnie opened the door and slipped through, stepping aside and ushering Sister and the other twin into the rest room on the left side of the hall. When the door closed the room was chimney dark and damp, smelled of ammonia and lye. Sister hovered close to Marnie, swaying with the baby in her arms, and sucked on her woolly coat while the other twin clung to Sister and whimpered.

"Hush, baby, hush," said Marnie in a shaky low voice.

They listened to the woman's shoes click on the hall floor, listened to the front door open and close and the key turn in the lock, and then they listened to the humming quiet of the library for what seemed like a long, long time.

That night in the library, in the warm and muzzy light, Marnie fed the children cheese crackers scavanged from a room in back. Then she read to them. She read what seemed like every single one of the shelved books Sister and the twins brought her; then they built a book tower and laughed when it tumbled down. She read about trains and trolls and a circus seal named Sam. She read to them in a soft night voice, rocking one of the twins on her lap. In the tiny red chair, she held the book high, knees spread so that her holey white panties showed beneath her flared gray skirt. She read them into a state of half sleep in which the twins coughed and turned on the wool rug next to the little round table. Then she went to the north end of the library and sat in a chair and read magazines and smoked till out in the night.

Sucking her thumb and listening to the furnace rattle and rasp, Sister watched her. Watched her read as she had never read before and would never read again.

Next morning Marnie went out, leaving the door wedged open with a book; she came back later with powdered doughnuts and chocolate milk, and then they played. Slept and played, and Marnie braided Sister's hair into a pigtail that stuck straight out. And Sister worked: She stamped as many books as she could manage—so many hours holed up with nothing else to do—for the library lady. She stamped till her hand cramped. (The twins dumped the slender box of evened-up checkout cards, but Sister was able to put most of them back.) Marnie sang to them while they peered out the windows and kissed the cold glass.

She went out and came back.

When they emerged early on Monday morning from the cocoon of the library, now littered with library cards, damaged books, food crumbs, cigarette butts, and bologna rinds like red rubber bands, the weather had warmed up like first spring and Marnie was Marnie again. Tough and untouchable, out to whip the gas man's butt.

~~~

Meanwhile at the café things have gotten rotten—rottener. Business has picked up, and Sister has found another petition on the door. The Methodists, this time. Oh, Lord! How . . . where will Sister go to church? It never occurs to her that she doesn't have to go at all, that nobody makes her. And she doesn't go because of her new quest for respect now. She just goes. And when Sunday rolls around, the first week of summer vacation, she strikes out for the Church of God, down a side road north of the schoolhouse.

"No," she tells Willa, "I don't believe I'll go to Sunday school at the Baptist church. I've just turned Church of God." Lies from a liar on her way to church. But she knows Willa knows—has to know. In a little place like Cornerville everybody knows. Is Willa sorry for Sister and the baby, Sister wonders? And knows she is, that the good lady isn't being friendly simply for the pleasure of Sister's company—Sister, who can teach her girls nasty tricks—or to keep the baby on weekends after having kept her all week long.

Once Sister opened a note sent from Willa to Marnie: "Please drop by and pay for babysitting. Two months behind." But now that school is out and Sister will be the baby-sitter, she expects Willa will forget it, so she throws away the note. Marnie might not need Willa next school term: With September such a long way off, Marnie could become respectable by then; Sister could be dead by then.

One thing about going to the Church of God: All the unpopular, poor girls from school go there, the ones who wear long skirts and buttoned-to-the-throat blouses, with uncut hair and scrubbed faces, so nobody shuns Sister. Oh, one or the other of the ladies might ask, "How's your mama doing, honey?" that kind of thing. But Sister can handle that: "Marnie's been praying and reading her Bible till out in the night. Soon as she gets her hair growed out, she's coming with me to church."

Besides, the twins had started following Sister to the Methodist church, and once they learned that the steeple contained a bell with a pull rope in the open vestibule, at their disposal twenty-four hours a day, they had remained faithful Methodists. Day and night, the bell tolls, and Sister finally knows where the twins are, what they are up to. If anybody else has caught on to who is ringing the bell, Sister hasn't heard. And she figures if they have, if the preacher and the whole Methodist church knows who, they can't very well confront the enemy, Marnie and Sade, to complain about their children.

~~~

The first dead-hot Sunday in June, Sister sets out for Sunday school and finds a partially burned cross stuck up in the spun gray dirt in front of the café. Glazy charred boards shocking her like curse words. She stops, considering it: The petitions were only warnings; this is a threat. Sister knows the stages of danger but not how to stop them. If she leaves the cross for Marnie and Sade to see, they might sell the café and get out of town. Huh-uh, not Marnie. Even if she is well on her way to hating the café—waitressing or whoring or whatever she's up to—one sure way to make her stay is somebody trying to make her go. Marnie don't take nothing off of nobody! Sister wants peace, if only temporary peace, and peace at this stage of danger is silence.

Sister tries to remember how old she was, where she was, when she saw her first burned cross. No, burning cross, and she was looking through a window with spider-web scratches and tiny bubbles that she tried to tap loose, to free, while watching Marnie in her nightgown waving her hands at the white-sheeted figures in the front yard. Yelling at them and then stomping back toward the house, but turning before she got there with her hands on her hips and mouthing off again. Day after day Marnie talked about taking on the KKK, but they never came back; Sister checked, and they never came back and the bubbles stayed trapped in the glass.

A few semis are parked along the shoulder of the road

from the café to the courthouse, but nobody is around. The trucks are idling with puffs of burned diesel on the smothery air, their drivers asleep behind the green-tinted windows. The truck before the café suddenly snorts like a dragon, then pulls away, roaring north to the traffic light, then down the dip at Troublesome Creek. Sister plucks the cross from the dirt, twists the stakes to overlap, and carries it to the scrub-oak-laced wire fence of the vacant lot between the Baptist church and the café and pitches it over into the briars.

The Methodist church bell rings.

One day Sister will be playing under the water sprinkler with the Lamar girls, then the next day she is tagging after Willa: putting up vegetables from her garden; scrubbing down the tongue-and-groove walls of the varicolored rooms; wringing chickens' necks in the pen out back, plucking, scalding, wrapping them for freezing; sunning mattresses on concrete blocks; scouring children in the washtub on the back porch. Then sitting cross-legged on the front porch with Willa, all perfumed and powdered and poised, as if she hasn't done a thing all day, waiting for Mr. Lamar to come home for supper from the turpentine woods on their farm near the Florida line.

Sister has decided that what she has to do is make people believe what they believe about Marnie isn't so. Make Marnie, and Sade, seem respectable. Or if not that, make herself look good for her new idol, Willa. Actually Sister looks more like Willa than her own girls do—well, not really, but her hair is dark like Willa's, and she might turn out pretty like Willa when she turns out; Willa's girls are blond and fair like their daddy. Sister glides in the screaking porch swing with the baby standing alongside, holding on to the back and watching Zelda the parakeet swing from her perch inside the cage.

The children are playing in the yard, chasing lightning bugs through the dusk, while *the grownups*, Sister and Willa, sit watch.

The church bell rings.

"Who you reckon would be doing that?" Willa says and stops rocking.

"I don't know," says Sister, swinging with her legs crossed at the knees.

They listen; the ringing stops.

"Guess some younguns playing." Willa rocks again.

"Probably."

Pat, with blond bangs and a ponytail, lifts her lantern of lightning bugs to the dusk, then marches around one of the oaks where the dark waits with Larry the Cat.

Earlier it had rained, and now a haze hangs in the starring sky, a clean, chill smell following the world's washing, like the wet of the inside walls after Willa's scrubbing.

"Marnie said tell you she'll be paying you soon," says Sister. "Café's doing better."

"Good." Willa slaps a yellowfly on her firm right calf.

"Seems like once a year, somebody tries to make a go of it with the old café."

"They're aiming to make it work." Sister turns in the swing and seats the baby on her leg, gazing at the lit square building up the highway. "That Sade's one smart business-man." In defense of Marnie's latest man, Sister has repeated verbatim Ray William's remark at church. Oh, well. "See all them cars and trucks yonder?" she adds. "All after Marnie's hamburgers."

"I bet."

Is Willa being snide? Sister checks her small dark face. "Used to, all them people would have to go to Valdosta for supper," says Sister.

"Well," says Willa, "I wish them all the luck."

Sister is in heaven. She has passed from brat stage to boss. She is Willa's friend, her confidante. But when Mr. Lamar's green pickup spirits into view through the haze along the south stretch of highway, and motors into the yard on the left side of the house, Willa is up and scurrying to the kitchen, lost to Sister.

"Wadn't that bad about that plane crashing over Grand Canyon?" Willa might say to Mr. Lamar, after not having said word one about a plane crash to Sister.

~~~

Sister stands on The Judge's brick walk. Fanning gnats with one hand and hoisting the baby on her cocked hip with the other. Burning up in the noon sun, on the bottom doorstep. Close as she can get without going up on the forbidden porch: one, from here, she can keep a lookout for Marnie at the café up the highway and make her getaway before her mama catches her where she's not supposed to be; and two, from here, Sister can get a good look at The Judge's ten-year-old granddaughter from Florida. She has a glass eye, and Willa has warned her girls not to stare, but Sister can't help it. She hates to defy Willa, but she just can't help it.

The glass-eyed girl is sitting with Neida and Alda on the wide board floor, middle of the porch, cutting paper dolls from a Sears Roebuck catalog. The Judge is sitting on the south end behind a screen of nooning morning glories, fanning and reading in fits and starts from a folded newspaper; June, whom Sister worshiped all last summer, is bogged serenely in a twig chair on the other end of the porch with her long tanned legs hooked over one arm. She is wearing white shorts and reading a clothbound blue book titled *The Search for Bridey Murphy*. Used to, on summer visits, she was queen of the neighborhood paper-doll gang, had a catalog bulging with precisely cut-out mamas and daddies and children—whole families. Now that she is sixteen, she has passed along her catalog to her cousin. The one with the freaky glass eye. The one who stood too close to a burning pile of trash and got blinded when glass popped out of the fire, but being rich and from Florida she got a glass eye that glitters and doesn't blink and can stare right at you and never see you staring back.

Or can it?

Sister steps closer for a better look, and the red-faced baby starts to whine and tries to wriggle free, which causes the girl with the glass eye to gaze at Sister. Sister steps into the shadow of the porch eave for a better look, but still cannot tell which is the glass eye. Both are blue with green light spokes, though the right eye does have yellow specks.

"'Steelworkers strike; get huge raise,'" reads The Judge. His long, scowling face lifts from the newspaper. "Lord in heaven help," he says, "everywhere you look it's communist." His black eyes settle on Sister, and she feels sure he has seen her touching up the president's picture. Then he says, "Why don't you bring that baby in out of the sun, gal? Put her down, let her ramble a bit."

Alda and Neida, with their backs to Sister and their fronts to the girl with the glass eye, hold up flashing silver scissors, then scoot over for Sister to join them in the nest of white paper trimmings and people. Some with cut-off hands and feet. Only June can cut out hands and feet.

Sister sets the baby free on the edge of the porch. She crawls on one knee and one foot to the screen door, peers inside where lazy clock ticks and smells of gingerbread radiate out, then crawls over to the rocker next to The Judge and pulls up with her wet diaper bagging on her bow legs.

Sister sits cross-legged in the circle of girls and again watches the girl with the glass eye, but just as she thinks she has picked out the eye that is glass, she has to jump up and gouge a red flower from the baby's mouth. The long clay pot full of geraniums, next to the morning glory screen, now looks like a bed of cactus-jointed green stalks with naked stems. Bitter smelling leaves and flowers lie wilting in the sun inching across the heart-pine floor.

When Sister looks again the girl with the glass eye is watching her—both eyes. They look the same. She lifts her straight sandy hair from her neck and blows at gnats swarming around the right eye. "Is that your baby?" she asks Sister.

"Baby sister," says Sister. "I just keep her."

"Every day?"

"Nearlybout."

June looks up from her book. "Sister's mama works at the café, Priss," she says.

"Oh, yeah," says the girl, "I remember. But I still don't see why we can't go there."

The Judge clears his throat and groans, and says, "Lord in heaven help." Same as always. Then rakes one age-scruffed hand through his young black hair.

Sister scoops up the baby, goes down the porch steps and across the hoed yard with its pecan trees and islands of dusky blue hydrangeas, white altheas, and scorched-rose sweet shrubs. And just to think, Sister had been on the verge of feeling sorry for that girl.

Willa, with store receipts and change multiplying in her white summer pocketbook, hands out nickels, dimes, and quarters to her girls for doing chores, or doing nothing. And when the traveling tent show stops over in Cornerville and sets up on the vacant lot behind Sirman's station and the café, Willa's pocketbook has spawned enough quarters for Sister a ticket too. Scrap of flesh that the baby is, she doesn't need a ticket as long as she sits on Sister's lap.

Saturday night double feature: *Zombies Walking* and *The Devil's Bride*. So scary your gums itch from gritting your teeth. So scary your bare toes root through the withy grass to the damp dirt. So scary you clutch Willa's home-fashioned wax paper cone of popped corn till it spills over the top. Movie projector whirring and beaming down the grass aisle, between the white and Negro sections of bleachers, producing a living stream of dust spects and bugs that you never knew were there, any more than you knew that dead people in the cemetery this side of the Alapaha River could rise up and start walking. Straight through locked doors if they have a mind to.

No backs on the long wooden bleachers, and your spine aches from stiffening before the second feature. You have to pee but hold it till you get home, because outside the tent the devil's bride could be roaming the woods with hoot owls and mean little boys. Like Paul and Mickey.

It is at the high point, just as the zombies are about to take over a city, just as Sister is about to find out if the beautiful woman with long black hair will make it to safety, that Paul and Mickey slide on their bellies under the left wall of the tent. Stoop-walking till they locate Sister, two bleachers from the front, on the left end, they scoot her over with Alda, Neida, Pat, and about a dozen other kids. All shuffling right, hissing and groaning, scattering popcorn and ticket stubs. The zombies freeze and the music fizzles and the bedsheet screen fades into never-was.

A yellow light flickers on from the pitch of the khaki tent, and the squat showman in a straw Panama hat and a green tucked shirt strolls up the middle aisle and across the front and down the left side and begins checking for ticket stubs.

"You go," he says to Mickey on the end now.

"You stay," he says to Paul, who is holding up Sister's ticket stub with the baby's single tooth print on it.

"You go," he says to Sister and the sleeping baby grafted to her chest: one body.

~~~

Midsummer, and just before the Ku Klux Klan is ready to come down on Marnie and Sade, so figures Sister, she gets a break. As the Bible says, "God will not put more on you than you can stand." And God sends the Firecracker Lady to set up her circus-of-sorts on the vacant lot before the wind has cleared the tent show's rubbish of paper popcorn cones and cola cups and orange ticket stubs in the tramped-down grass limning out where the tent was pitched.

Staked front and center of the Baptist church, a brown baboon paces round and round, with his chain stretched tight and his red-flared behind shining, just in time for Wednesday night prayer. Back-to-back cages, on a flatbed truck, exhibit a seething-eyed lion sprawled house-cat-like with his paws crossed, and a black bear with a burnished ruff, which scuttles night and day as if searching for an opening in the rusty bars; and best of all the Firecracker Lady in striped socks and black, heeled sandals who lives in an Airstream travel trailer with a twenty-four-foot boa named "Love."

The churches seem to forget Sade's Café and start circulating petitions to get rid of the Firecracker Lady and her fireworks stand and Love.

Bible school has gone berserk, with all the children scattering, alternately spooking the baboon and trying to sneak a peep at Love, the boa.

Customers, mostly men, from the café stop to buy firecrackers and tease the lion, the bear, and the baboon. Some hint at a sex sideshow with the boa. In other words Sodom and Gomorrah have arrived in Cornerville.

The quick, wiry woman with black stone eyes is a Gypsy—a Gypsy!—and when Ray Williams, now county commissioner, and his gang call, she tells them her rights: She has rented the lot from Mr. King and can do as she damn well pleases. Mr. King, ornery and sure, claims he had no idea her circus would cause such a ruckus: "Get your asses off my property!" Sade and Marnie reap the harvest sown by the Firecracker Lady.

And Sister glories in having somebody in Cornerville

who is beneath her. Somebody else to take the heat. Even talks bad about the Firecracker Lady and her housefly-drawing pets to Willa, who merely goes on about her business of wringing chickens' necks and scrubbing walls and children. The Firecracker Lady will pass, Willa says, and swats a fly.

But before she passes, Cornerville is a bloom and blaze of fireworks, Love becomes a legend in the study of perversity, and the baboon gets loose.

Always at the mercy of everybody picking at him—damaged, shrunken, and cowering in his dirt circle—the baboon is now a monster on the prowl.

Early Saturday, Sister gets up, fights with the twins, and heads out for the Lamar house to fill the baby's bottle with raw milk from Willa's cow in the pen south of the house. When Sister gets to the highway, ready to cross the heat-drawing asphalt, she sees Alda, Neida, and Pat knotted in the front door.

"Run!" they yell. "Baboon's on the loose."

Sister shifts the baby on her hip and dashes across the highway and up on the porch. "What you mean 'on the loose'?"

"He broke the chain last night."

Sister wedges through the door to the cool green living room. "Where is he?"

"We don't know." Neida, pudgy and blond in green shorts and a cropped shirt, slams the wooden door and leans on it.

"You girls, come on and eat breakfast," Willa calls from the yellow kitchen at the rear of the house. The house, built by Willa and her husband, is two rooms wide, with a longish kitchen from which two other bedrooms branch off. And between the bedrooms, a bathroom-in-progress, which Sister loves and which makes her think the Lamars are rich: white porcelain fixtures with sawdust and tape and tools instead of water, but the day will come when the sea-blue paint will completely cover the narrow tongue-and-groove walls, floating white soap and white towels and the sucking noise of the toilet and the drains that could carry you to China, where the girls sometimes try to dig to with spoons in the backyard.

Sister checks Willa's small, tanned face to see if she is scared but can't tell. She is smiling, as usual, while scrubbing a pot at the counter under the side-set old mullions on the south wall. But the fact that she doesn't go out to milk that morning tells that, if not scared, she is leery of the baboon.

"Sheriff said he was gone shoot him," says Neida. The girls slide onto the bench at the slick white kitchen table, left side of the swinging door to the living room.

"Why would he shoot him?" says Pat.

"Why you think?" says Alda. "That baboon's liable to kill somebody for chunking stuff at him."

"Girls, eat," says Willa. "Feed the baby some of that oatmeal, Sister. She doesn't need to be drinking Kool-Aid first thing in the morning."

The nerves in Sister's kneecaps jump—a baboon on the loose! She dips some gelled oatmeal into a bowl and spoons it to the baby's mouth. Up till now Sister has been enjoying the baboon and the Firecracker Lady being the focus of the town's attention. Now she is scared. Like everybody else she has paraded just out of the baboon's reach, taunting him. His wrinkled brown face like the face of a coconut. If she were him, she would . . .

All afternoon Sister and the Lamar girls traipse from window to window throughout the sunny house: They gaze out the single window of Alda's and Neida's blue middle room, and up into the branches of Miss Willington's moss-swagged live oaks; they perch on the little bed in Pat's little side room, where Larry the Cat sleeps, and study the brittle old barn and loft that blocks their view of Miss Willington's house and chicken pen and tractor shelter; they stake out before the four windows in Willa's pink room on the front with neck-yanking glances at the mysterious second door to the porch; they kneel on the green couch and chairs in the green living room and canvass the hedges in the yards of the two white houses to the left of Sister's lane—they quick-check Sister's lane with its confusion of hiding places at the end—and the Lamar's pecan grove south of the house; and across the highway, in The Judge's patch of red calla lilies, they watch for the baboon's red-flared behind to pop up in the picture. The baboon could be anywhere. He could be hunkered down in the unstirred dust beneath the house, this very minute. Under the very spots where they are rooted with sucked-in breath. Half hoping he will show, half hoping he won't.

The church bell rings around three o'clock, and Alda says she has read that a church bell ringing in the middle of the week is a signal that trouble has started or stopped, and the bell ringing now probably means that the baboon has been caught.

Sister knows better, knows it is the twins ringing the bell, should tell but doesn't. She lets Willa, her best friend and only living soul in the world who values her, walk all the way over to the Firecracker Lady's trailer to ask, and doesn't tell, and hates herself, because if Willa gets mauled to death by the baboon it is Sister's fault.

Sister watches through the blue-room window as Willa, in a pink sun dress and bare feet, crosses the sun-streaked highway, peering up into the live oaks, then vanishes into the Airstream trailer this side of Sirman's station. Comes out again and starts for the house.

"Hurry, hurry," Sister whispers. "Don't die."

When Willa comes through the back door, Sister is sitting on the kitchen floor with the girls, cutting paper dolls from a Sears Roebuck catalog. Pat jumps up, squealing. "Is he caught? Is he caught yet? Can we go out now?" The baboon's escape is no longer entertainment but punishment.

"Nope, not yet." Willa goes to the kitchen table, covered in stiff, line-dried clothes, and begins sprinkling shirts and pants and dresses, rolling them up and placing them in a basket on the floor. When she gets done, she sets up the wooden-legged board and plugs in the iron, testing the heat with spit on her finger. Then she irons over a sheet of wax paper to make the surface glide. On the first shirt she bears down with the iron, making the sheet-covered board creak. The air in the kitchen smells hot—melted wax and ironed starch—and *is* hot.

"Mother," says Alda, "Sister's crying."

"No, I'm not," says Sister, sniffling. Maybe she is, maybe she isn't. Maybe she has a cold. It's none of their business.

"What's the matter, Sister?" says Willa and parks the iron on a flat metal plate.

"I've got to get home," says Sister, and scoops up the baby with a fistful of paper and starts out the front.

"Sister," Willa calls out, but Sister keeps walking, walking, straight across the highway without even looking, up the lane in the heat that seems textured of the locusts' hum, toward the house under the tight growth of trees with monkey faces of knotholes and into the yard with the junk cars she hardly sees anymore. She is halfway across the porch before she spies the baboon's brown coconut face in the jungle of black gums. She stares at him, he stares at her. She goes inside and cries to the baby for a change.

*I*T IS SUNDAY, AND ON SATURDAY
Sade has gotten the bill from Sirman's station for charged
bubble gum and Nehi's and Popsicles and Zero bars,
amounting to fifty-one dollars and eighty-two cents—"A
frigging fortune, and by God, somebody's gonna pay!"—
meaning hide, thinks Sister. Not him. Not Sade Odums who
works from can to can't and then gets home to find that one
of Marnie's brats has to be picked up in Phoenix City,
Alabama. Sade's only day off, Sunday. And how come
Mickey to be hiding out in the sleeper of a semi anyhow?

Sade parades through the house, beating his broad
blond chest like an ape, while Sister stays with the baby in
her overcast room, lit by the sunny blond bedroom suite,
and Paul sits on the front doorsteps with his head hung,
lost without his twin, whom he dared to sneak into the
semi—he might never see his brother again. Marnie
whines and bluffs and dodges Sade in the path from the
kitchen to the living room.

"Dammit, Marnie!" says Sade. "You ain't raising nothing but a bunch of hellions." It is as if the children have just caught his notice.

"Me! Me?" Marnie sounds like she is singing. "Who cooks and entertains eighteen out of twenty-four hours a day, at whose café?" Her brown eyes spark in her white face, which doesn't go with her dyed-black hair.

"Don't tell me you don't like doing it," says Sade, wheeling in his white socks. "Don't tell me you don't get a kick out of flirting with the men."

"Flirting! With that bunch of hicks!" She has her hands on her hips, her crooked nose flaring. "Just because I've let myself go doesn't mean I'd stoop to that. And besides, you knew I had children when you took up with me, and whose idea was it to pick up extra business by . . . ?"

They get low, then loud, low again, loud again.

Sister knows before they are done they will have back-tracked over their entire approximate two years together—sometimes he'd leave, sometimes she'd leave, and sometimes they'd bump heads leaving at the same time; Sister knows they will backtrack over every other fight and each other's shortcomings till they hardly recollect what started this fight in the first place. Might even forget about Mickey in Phoenix City, Alabama. She wishes she could go with Sade to get Mickey but doesn't know for sure if Sade will go. She crosses her fingers and hopes that Marnie, who has let herself go to fat, still has the power to persuade him.

The church bell rings—for real, this time—and Sister

starts to get ready for Sunday school, can almost taste the peace of the crude Church of God with its cool concrete floor and tinny piano. But if she goes, Sade and Marnie might forget about Mickey. She hears the dry leaves rustling outside her window and stands with the baby to see Paul wandering toward the woods with his head down, arms limp alongside. He is wearing a skimpy brown-striped shirt and khaki shorts. His crewcut hair looks khaki too, his face khaki—connected freckles.

Marnie and Sade are fussing in their bedroom, next to Sister's, and in a few minutes, Sister hears smacked flesh and Marnie crying, then Sade stomping from the house. After he has started his pickup and sped up the lane, Sister goes into the living room and stares out the window at the Lamar house, still and Sunday-somber under the oaks. She could go over there and beg Willa to go to Alabama for Mickey, but if Willa drives, Sister doesn't know of it. She wouldn't ask Mr. Lamar because she doesn't really know him. She wouldn't ask him because . . . well, just because he's a man. But to her knowledge only men drive—except for Marnie, whose Ford Victoria has a flat—only men have cars or trucks, so she tries to go over a list of men in her head—mostly those on the Baptist petition—to decide who she might ask.

But while changing the baby's diaper—adding another to the heap of dirty ones on the floor by the green vinyl couch—it occurs to her that Mickey is no worse off in Alabama than in Georgia, that when he was home he was on his own, just as he is there. Besides, maybe Sade has gone after him. Sister no longer hears Marnie crying, so she tiptoes to her bedroom door, listening before she opens it. Marnie is sprawled facedown on the dingy, bunched sheets, asleep.

When Marnie wakes up, around three that afternoon, she isn't talking. She is swift but sullen and silent. She airs her red nylon dress on a wire hanger from one of the front-porch rafters, shampoos her dead-black hair, and has Sister trim it. She even cleans out a trail through the house—clothes, toys, trash. She plays the green boxy radio loud. Bulletin: A storm system is moving west to east. Then more country music. Sitting on the left edge of the porch, Marnie brushes the baby's clear white hair and gathers a sprig on the crown with a pink ribbon. The baby looks like a damaged doll. Then Marnie tries to teach her to say "Mama." But the baby only gnaws on the handle of the hairy brush and crawls toward Sister on the doorsteps.

"Don't let her get messed up," says Marnie and gets up and strolls through the open front door.

When she comes out again, she is wearing her shiny blue swimsuit with the foam breast pads, her wet black hair like braided yarn on her fleshy, white shoulders. Carrying a yellow blanket, she goes down the doorsteps to a sunny spot in the yard, next to her lopsided blue-and-white Ford Victoria, and spreads the blanket and lies on her back. Off-again on-again sun through patches of eastward-rushing clouds and gusts of wind that lift the corners of the yellow blanket and carry the hushed sounds of Sunday in Cornerville. Georgia dirt and gnats, hated by Marnie, surround Marnie in her shiny blue swimsuit.

Sister wonders if Marnie is getting in shape to leave Sade—sunning her marbled-fat thighs usually means that she is getting ready to reduce them—if she is scheming her next move, her next man. Surely she must believe that Sade has gone after Mickey; otherwise she'd be out trying to get him herself. Used to, she would have. Used to, even if she had a flat on the car, she would have wheedled, or whored, or done what she had to do to go after one of her children. If for no other reason save pity or pride.

The baby scoots around Sister on the porch steps and almost topples headlong to the dirt; Sister gasps and grabs her by her diaper waist. And then it comes to Sister, in the same eye-opening manner as the respect thing, that the baby has never been named. That particularly in a crisis, the baby should have a name to be called by.

"Marnie," Sister says and scoops up the baby and heads for Marnie's blanket, sitting next to her long white feet.

"What?" Marnie doesn't move. Seems to be concentrating on the sun to make it shine longer between clouds.

"We gotta name the baby," says Sister. "She's nearbout a year old, and we ain't named her."

"Nothing's hit me yet." Marnie lifts her head and shields her eyes with one hand.

"Well, we'll just go on and name her then," says Sister. "Anything's better than nothing."

Marnie sits up, cocking her knees, and studies the baby on Sister's lap. "Looks like a Lily to me."

The baby grins, her one-and-only tooth shining like bone punched through her red gums.

"Lily," says Sister, lifting the baby so that her scrawny legs dangle like a crane's. The sun at the baby's back makes her look sheer as skimmed milk. "Look," Sister says to Marnie, "you can just about see through her."

"Well, I declare," says Marnie. "Shh," she says and listens toward the deejay's lively jabbering on the radio inside the house.

Then, "Some women have all the luck."

"What women?" Sister asks.

"That movie star, Grace Kelly—they say she's marrying a prince."

"Did Sade go after Mickey?"

"Said he was." Marnie lies down again with one arm over her eyes. "Said he wadn't too."

Suddenly Sister feels mad: Marnie couldn't care less if the storm sweeping west to east blows them all away, if Sister dies before school starts in September, if the baby has a name or not. She just settled for the first thing popped to mind, and it is clear that she doesn't care about Mickey, who might already be blown away by the storm, which could have passed through Alabama by now.

"You don't give a damn, do you?" Sister says low—not

really meaning for Marnie to hear, not meaning for Marnie not to hear either.

Marnie props on one elbow, staring at Sister as if seeing her for the first time.

———

That night Sister lies awake till she hears Sade's pickup come roaring down the lane—long past midnight—till she hears him stomp in, a single set of footsteps that means no Mickey yet. In bursts of lightning that ignite the mirror of her dresser, at the foot of her bed, she dreads the stalking thunderclaps and the rain that seems never to come, but when it does, seems always to have been there. Pecking the tin overhead like beaked monsters. And then she lets go, dreaming of white lilies on a field of snow. Hearing only herself breathing—a lump—and knowing it is her. Her body just a cloudy gray mass, darkness behind her eyes. Alone in the world: The Sister seen through Marnie's eyes as if for the first time.

———

When Sister wakes the next morning, the house is still and quiet, sun shining through the window over the blond headboard that halfway covers the opening. She lies still, listening to the dry click of grasshoppers in the dead leaves, trying to sort reasons for the lull in the usual racket of the house.

She knows that Marnie and Sade have gone to the café, which means they have made up, and remembering that Mickey is in Alabama, she figures now that Sade's routine week has begun, he won't go after him till next Sunday. If at all.

In a few minutes she hears Paul in the kitchen, mewling like a kitten, and then the baby in the living room rattling the bars of her crib.

Sister gets up, stripping off the white T-shirt she sleeps in, and slips on her red shorts and shirt at the foot of the bed (before she became respectable, she used to sleep in her clothes to keep from having to change the next morning, especially during summer, especially when she was sleepy). She slides open the cabinet door on one end of her shelf headboard, takes out two of the three Zero candy bars she had charged at Sirman's station and carries them to the kitchen.

Paul is sitting at the table with his head on his arms, stifling crying. Houseflies buzz and light on food-crusted dishes. The table is centered in a chute of sunlight from the east window with its punched-out screen. Sister taps Paul's bony arm with one of the candy bars. "Here," she says. "Eat this."

He looks up, takes it, then shucks the paper from the frosty white bar. But after the first bite, he starts crying again, freckled face suffusing and knitting with grief.

Sister sits across from him, eyeing him over an open loaf of moldy white bread with slices fanned onto the tabletop. "You know Sade'll go get him," she says, munching her own candy. "Marnie'll make him, you know she will."

"Yeah," he says sullenly, "but *when*?"

"Soon as he gets a break."

"Then how come he didn't do it yesterday?"

Sister shrugs, gnawing a sugary corner of the malt candy bar.

"I tell you how come." Paul sinks his too-big top teeth into the bar. "Cause he likes to make us suffer, that's how come."

"Mickey's probably having a big time."

The baby in the living room rattles the crib slats and squeals. Her way of saying, "I'm up."

"You don't know nothing." Paul wads the candy wrapper and throws it at Sister's right shoulder. It ricochets to the heap of cans and bottles and paper next to the gummy white stove. The whole room smells rotten, like week-old flower water in a vase.

"Okay, so he's dead," says Sister. That's what it feels like to her, like Mickey is dead.

Paul starts crying again, gets up, kicking odd shoes and dirty clothes along the trail from the table to the back screen door. Slams out.

The baby squeals twice.

"Okay, Lill," yells Sister, swallowing her last bite of candy. "Lill," that's what she will call the baby; "Lily" is too old-timey.

Sister pours a bottle of Willa's cow's milk from one of the glass jugs in the refrigerator, then goes to Lill in the moldy-pink living room and lifts her from the crib. Lill sucks while Sister changes her diaper on the green couch. The folds of her groin are reddish-purple from diaper rash. Sister knows she should wipe her with a wet rag—maybe scrounge up some baby powder—but she doesn't want to take the time. She honestly has no idea what she will do, how she will get Mickey home, but knows she will make some kind of arrangement before the day is over. She will put being respectable on hold, and as proof of her determination and her break with respectability for the day, she leaves the house without her sandals.

When she sets out with the baby, the sun is already moving toward its pitch in the high blue sky, raying along the lane from the background of black gums to the white front of the Lamar house. At the highway, starting to cross, Sister hears their back screen door screak open and clap shut and the girls laughing. Turning right, toward Cornerville, she sees Willa hanging clothes on the line in the deep backyard bordered by pine woods.

No, not Willa. It will have to be a man; it will have to be Ray Williams who goes after Mickey. He's the one who took the call to the courthouse from the semi driver in Alabama, and except for Sade, he is the only one who will know where to go in Phoenix City, Alabama.

Two pickups are parked in front of the café, and Sister has to tip along the hot, tarry edge of the highway to get around them. The baby has finished her bottle, and after a couple of dry sucks, yanks it from her milky lips and lets go. Sister stops, watching it roll in the gravel-laced sand and beneath the bed of one of the trucks.

"Now what you gone do when you get hungry?" she says. And suddenly she realizes how mad she is at Sade. How much she dreads facing Ray Williams and begging him to go after Mickey. How afraid she is that Mickey could be in trouble. She tells herself that if the truck driver was a bad man, he wouldn't have called the courthouse in the first place. Mickey will be fine till next Sunday, she decides, and decides to go to Hoot Walters's store instead, see if he'll let her have some food on credit. No more candy, which she can still taste thick on her tongue. Just food that she has to have, just enough to get by on. Sade shouldn't fuss about that.

But when she sees Paul walking alone down the dip of Troublesome Creek, north of the crossing, she cuts across the oak-shady courtyard and heads toward the front of the courthouse. White, two-story, with windows like doors and a long, hollow hall that smells of dust, mold, and old paper, twists of tobacco smoke from the open office doors that give off solemn voices and the clack of typewriters, an odor of justice seeping from the dusky old wainscoting and music in the retelling of ancient records, land deeds, and births and deaths. Who did what to whom—the how, when, and where of it.

The worst Ray Williams can say is no. Sister has heard

that before, and what has it cost her? But that was before pride, before she knew what pride was and how damning it can be. She looks down at her feet, at her dirt-pied toes, and keeps walking till she hears from one of the open doors near the end of the hall Ray Williams's mock-gruff voice. When she gets to the door, she looks in and sees him sitting on the right corner of his desk with one elevated black shoe swinging. He is talking into a black telephone and fanning his tapered face with some stapled white papers, either pretending not to see Sister or making her wait.

Then finally: "Well, if it's not Sister," he says, and places the receiver of the phone on its base. "That baby's getting bigger than you are. Y'all get your boy back yet?"

Sister sets the baby on the left corner of the desk and circles her tubelike body with her arms. "Nosir, we ain't."

"What! Sade couldn't find him?"

"Didn't go, I don't guess."

"Hum." He gets up and steps behind his desk and settles into his cradle-back chair. "Well, tell Sade he might better get on over there." He rears, rocks, latches his hands behind his head. "Law in Alabama's liable to take a youngun running loose like that."

"You don't reckon?"

"I know so." He sits forward, prying open a paper clip, fashioning a hook. "Hear tell they'll just turn younguns like that over to the state. That's what they do with runaway boys."

"He didn't run away."

"All the same to them." He eyes her through his black-rimmed glasses with the clip-on shades tilted up. "They don't ask."

"I was wondering if I might could get you to go pick him up."

He draws his elbows back on the chair arms, tapping the dark scratched wood with his fingernails, watching Sister, watching the baby trying to reach behind for a bottle of ink.

"Figgered you'd know right where to pick Mickey up," Sister says, "and you got a car and all."

"Costs for gas." He places one finger on his pink bunched lips. "Besides, I was just getting used to a little peace. Church bells go off now, it means church." He swivels the chair to stare out the doorlike window at the red-brick church next to the white post office with its steep cobalt roof.

"I could make him and Paul stay away from the church from now on." Sister stands the baby on the desk, still holding her around the waist, to keep her from bothering the ink bottle.

"Pshaw, gal!" Williams turns again, eyeing her again. "You can't handle them boys, you know that."

"I can." She feels hopeful now, hopeful and back on course—her usual begging, loafing self. And uses it. "I can make 'em do what I want 'em to do."

"Well, like I say," he says, getting up and packing his blue shirt into his navy pants, "gas ain't free."

"I ain't got no money, but I can work it out if you got something needs doing." She looks around his office: green filing cabinet, two straight chairs, cardboard boxes of junk—dusty and disarrayed, but not nasty.

"I bet you can," he says and laughs, "I bet you can. You got enough of your mama in you to do that."

The soft black hair on Sister's arms stiffens, remembering his insinuation at church. She will handle all that later.

"Office don't need cleaning," he says. "But you know my li'l ol' fish camp, back there behind the cemetery on the river? Well, I been meaning to hire some woman to go in there and clean up. Had a big fish fry when I was 'lectioneering for county commission."

She picks up the baby, feeling the comforting warmth of her naked chest. Her heart beating against Sister's heart.

"You up to that?" He grins.

"Yessir." She knows she's either just sold herself or lied. And then a light comes on in her head. "When you get back from Alabama, I'll have that place spic and span," she says.

"Huh-uh." He walks around the desk, cracking his knuckles. "Can't let younguns go out there without me. Might fall in the pond and get drowned and me not there."

The light in Sister's head goes out.

"Couldn't take that risk atall," he says.

"Yessir."

"Honey," he says, clapping her shoulder and shaking it, "your baby brother's good as home."

She clutches the baby so tight she grunts and starts to leave.

But he steps in front of her, shaking a hair-tufted finger in her face. "But I'm gone be looking for you to be at that fish camp tomorrow. Right after dinner, you hear?"

He seems to read her mind and turns mean. No smile. "And if you ain't, I'm gone have your little brothers put in foster homes. Ain't a soul in Cornerville don't know for a fact they been running the road. And that baby there too. Ain't half the time got no clothes on to speak of."

Sister's tongue feels scummy. She clutches the baby tighter and waits for him to threaten sending her off too. When he doesn't, she takes it for a sign of something worse.

NOW THAT MICKEY IS SAFE at home and everybody is free to forget the Alabama episode—everybody, that is, except Sister—she wonders whether her brother is worth her sacrifice. A sacrifice she doesn't yet know what it is.

It is morning again, Tuesday, D day for Sister, and God has cursed the world with sunshine (if only it would rain, she wouldn't have to go to the fish camp). Not the bitter sun of yesterday that had burned on the tin roof, baking Sister and Lill. Rotting butcher paper and shit diapers perfuming the airless house. Lill whiny, sweaty. Her bottle is gone.

On Monday Sister had started to Willa Lamar's to get milk and to ask if she had a bottle to fit the spare nipple and ring found under the couch. At first Sister thought that Lill might starve without her bottle; then she reasoned that if the baby was old enough to sip milk from a cup, she shouldn't need a whole bottle of milk to survive.

Finally Lill had whined herself to sleep in her crib, her

whine amplified by the churning blades of Sade's electric fan, and Sister was left alone with the mushrooming dread of meeting Ray Williams at his fish camp the next day. When she thought she could no longer bear the heat, a thunderstorm came rolling in out of the west, rain beating on the tin like acorns in fall, and cooled the house under a dark tent of clouds. Terrified of the lightning, she had scrunched between a stuffed brown chair and the baby's crib, ready to yank Lill up and run if the next spear of lightning should set the house on fire. While the sky boomed, she tried to imagine what would happen at the fish camp with Ray Williams. She knew she would go, and she knew she would do what he said. She even knew it would be sex and what sex was, though she had no definition to go with the images in her head.

Sex was walking off into the woods as she'd once seen Marnie do with an old mechanic who kept up her Ford Victoria. Sister and the twins waiting in the hot car next to the tobacco barn where Marnie was working, and listening to the other hands talk and laugh—"That Marnie, she something! That gal sho' pay her debts." Or sex was Marnie sending Sister out to play when the man came to collect the rent while they were living in Jasper, Florida. Or crouching at Marnie's bedroom door during a storm, like now, while Marnie and her man squeaked the bedsprings and moaned like trapped wind in a chimney.

Since Sister had learned what was going on at the café, she'd put two and two together, how Marnie had been bargaining with her body all along. Whatever men and women did, Sister figured, felt good to the man but not to the woman, because if it had been good for the woman she would be charged for sex too. Would have nothing to bargain with.

Sister's knees ached from hugging them to her chest. Lightning streaked window to window of the living room, the fan quit. The absence of the whirring, a terrifying lapse in the ongoing racket of rain. She had wondered where Paul was, but wasn't worried because wherever he was he would find some place to get in out of the storm.

And that line of thinking set her to reasoning again that Mickey in Alabama could fend for himself till Ray Williams got there.

Tomorrow. A way out. Was there a way out? No. She would just grit her teeth and do what she had to. It wouldn't kill her. She hoped. If she didn't go, Lill, whose silvery head wedged against the spokes of the crib, would go to a foster home. Would she be better off? All Sister knew was she couldn't bear to let Lill and the twins go, that there was something helpless and sad about them that made her love them. Even when she hated the twins, at the high point of her hate, she could look at their bony pale rib cages and see Jesus nailed on the cross.

With the cool following the rain came the mosquitoes, a hulled whine that set her teeth on edge. That night she lay in her bed till the dark was as thick as the frogs' throbbing in the woods and waited for Mickey to get home.

When he still hadn't come by midnight—always announced by Marnie and Sade coming in—she felt almost relieved. She listened to dogs barking off in the quarters till she fell asleep and woke while it was still dark to the clap of a car door and the car driving away. Still, she lay there listening to Mickey tipping in, going into his bedroom, beyond her south wall, him and Paul talking and snickering till they fell asleep, and then listened to the nothingness ring of relief and dread.

~~~

For something to think about while Sister changes Lill to go to the fish camp on Tuesday morning, she entertains herself with notions of Sade and Marnie not discovering that Mickey is home till they close the café for Sunday, then finding he has been home since last Monday night. She tries imagining them glad, then mad, making it out the door and up the lane with that disaster-turned-celebration picture in her head.

Willa, sweeping her front walk, speaks to Sister and stands holding her corn broom as Sister turns from the lane and heads uptown without a word. Sister knows she should leave Lill with Willa, but somehow a baby riding her hip means limitations with her body.

Her shinbones ache from walking with her knees locked. When her mind wanders from the ironic situation of Marnie and Sade not discovering Mickey home till Sunday, she snaps the image back, just as she used to do in anticipation of Santa Claus. And she can say one thing for Marnie: She always makes sure the children have Christmas, whether she has to whore or waitress for toy money. Marnie loves to tell about the people she met while working at the S&K Steakhouse in Valdosta: two men, brothers, who told her about how one of them almost died in a car wreck because the other had quit believing in God, and at the point of his brother's near death, the unbelieving brother began believing in God, and his brother pulled through.

Passing through the valley of the shadow of death, along the fork from 129 to 94, behind the broken string of downtown stores, Sister shortcuts to the cemetery where she used to play hide-and-seek behind the headstones before she found out about pride and respect and had to quit playing, and none of it makes sense, not even the fact of Lill having to be weaned from her bottle and her so young, so small, just as Sister is being weaned from playing to get respect, which she is now giving up and which probably never was all that important in the first place.

Who looks? Who cares that she is now marching toward the fish camp behind the cemetery to have sex with a man older than her daddy, whom she hasn't seen in close to three years; when he had come he'd ended up quarreling with Marnie about child support and who she was going with at the time.

Sister crosses Highway 94, shifting Lill to her other

hip, hot tar burning in her nostrils and heat shimmering before her eyes. Ears buzzing with locusts and dread. She can see the cemetery on the hill, sterile sand and white stone set against the green woods of the riverbanks, all under a blue sky with a scatter of cottony clouds. And goes on walking along the shoulder, walking because to stop she might turn around or cross that strip of beggarweeds to the foot-trodden path where a row of small frame houses are set back from the highway, where an old woman fans on her front porch and children dart about the run-together yards: Help. But nobody sees Sister walking to her doom. Slipping past like downhill water.

At the ramp leading into the cemetery, she stops, gazing longingly at the concrete Alapaha River bridge, which, if crossed, would carry her west out of Cornerville. What if she should keep walking, she and Lill? What if they hitched a ride into Valdosta and found a place to stay? They might starve; they might be picked up and put in foster homes.

She turns down the two-path road along the east end of the cemetery, fleshy green prickly pears with thorns, and trashed flowers from the graves along the fencerow of scrub oaks. And over the fence a field of crimson wildflowers, smooth as paint in the still air. The sun draws on the grass-knitted sand of the graveyard and glints off the headstones like shooting stars.

When she reaches the shade of hollies and oaks on the north end of the cemetery, passing through the open wire gate to the fish camp, she can hear water rilling over the spillway. A song that stays in her head. She follows the road into the camp, where sunlight through the thick stand of trees flocks the cool packed sand. Nobody in sight, no sound but locusts humming and frogs thrumming and water. A square screened shelter sits to the left of the pond, which covers half the camp, with a spillway at the other end where Troublesome Creek tumbles sun-shot water from the woods to the brink, spouting a line of water into the inky pool. She scans the planes and swells of shadows about the camp for the lean, youngish body of old Ray Williams, for any movement, but the only motion is the sudden swaying shadows in the whispery breeze of the pines, which seem to make up from the water rushing over the spillway. A wood-pecker pecks the trunk of a cypress, a rapid *ta-ta-tat-tat*, sending shivers over the water and Sister's flesh.

By the time she gets to the screened shed, she has decided that, after all, Ray Williams had really meant for her to clean up and nothing else. She is so relieved that the salt of dread on her tongue turns to sugar—a taste she has learned not to trust. One last look around—the calm of crickets singing, the willow-tart scent of water, and the strangled chirruping of frogs—and she opens the screened door and steps inside. A lizard flashes across one of the four rough-lumber tables, set two to each side of the doorway.

She sets Lill on the ridged concrete floor, in a runner of sunlight, and goes to the boxy white kerosene stove along the back wall. Among the clutter of lard cans and flour and cornmeal sacks, and a bag of sugar turned to stone, on the wall-length shelf above the stove-and-sink set, she finds two greasy pot lids and takes them to Lill. She clanks them together and grins, and in the after-ring of racket Sister flushes from her scalp to her toes.

"Don't do that," she says, her voice sweeping out like the sweep of water along the spillway to the right of the screened-in room. If she hurries, if she really hurries and cleans, really cleans, she can always claim she has done exactly what she said she'd do. Will it matter? Will he come? Will she owe him later, regardless? She can try. She can try. Maybe he hadn't meant what she'd thought in the first place. Maybe she simply has a dirty mind, like Sueann Horton's mama said in the first place.

She turns on the spigot over the chipped white sink, rusty water trickling onto stiff wadded rags and clumps of gelled grits. After she has softened one of the rags till it grows rancid and limp, she dumps some soap powder onto it and begins scrubbing the grease-cankered stove; a gray smear like storm clouds emerges.

She rinses the rag and adds more soap and begins scouring again, listening to the baby clank the lids and the rushing song of water and locusts.

She keeps glancing behind at the shady road that leads from the cemetery, waiting; not turning her back, not for a minute, because she knows that trick—somebody sneaking up from behind. But now and then she forgets, while wiping down the small white refrigerator and wiping the tables, and wheels with a start, expecting him when she remembers. Only the trill of water and the on-again off-again wailing of frogs. She isn't fooled. He will come. He will come just as he said, if only to keep children from falling in the pond and not to mess with them.

Once she has to stop cleaning to rescue Lill from the soot-feathered brick fireplace and almost wishes Ray Williams *would* come—where is he? Her neck stings from jerking her head around. But nothing. She is almost done. Almost hopeful. Sweeping the corduroy concrete floor around the long benches and tables, she spies another lizard flashing along one of the screen ledges with its red flag out.

A fish rises on the pond, wobbling the brown water.

Now that she is finished, almost free now, she can't resist looking back at the neat room with pride and courage born of relief.

She kisses Lill on her sooty cheek and hurries along the road toward the open gate, up the shady lane, faster, faster, and scans the stark sand of the cemetery, the heat-bleached tombstones. Free.

Then she spots Ray Williams's blue car turning in at the cemetery ramp, slow moving in the wavery heat rays and dreamlike, his head a darkened lightbulb behind the sun-sparked windshield, and, as the car comes, taking on light till the smooth features of his hatchet face extinguish even the sun.

He brakes when he gets to her. "Thought I wadn't coming, huh?"

He props one arm in the window and stares out, grinning. His green-tinted clip-on sunshades pick up her reflection.

"I'm done through."

"That so?" He sucks air through his longish teeth, sticks one arm out the window, and gooses Lill in the ribs. She flinches and looks away as if she is twenty years old and snubbing him.

"Yessir," says Sister, stepping aside. "I'm through."

"Well, I guess you and me better go back and have a little look-see." He leans across the seat to open the opposite door for her to get in.

While he is busy with the door, Sister trots with the baby bobbing in her arms along the east fence of the cemetery, parallel to the cemetery road. Dodging prickly pears and wooden spikes from dead flower arrangements, she wrenches around to see the blue car easing on up the cemetery road, toward the camp, and figures Williams is either searching for a place to turn around and come back and chase her down or is letting her go. The baby squeals and laughs with each jolt.

"Shh!" says Sister and edges closer to the rusty wire fence, ready to hop over into the field of felt crimson flowers if Williams comes after her. When she gets to the corner post, near the cemetery ramp, she takes the path along the row houses fronting the highway, never slowing till she gets to the crossing in Cornerville.

Her breathing is jagged and asthmatic and keeps tune

with her soles rasping on the hot pavement. Crossing to the courtyard railing, she watches for peeps of the blue car between the buildings on the other side of Highway 129.

A pulpwood truck with a dome of poles is parked on the corner before the red-and-white gas pump at King's filling station, smells of raw resin, hot rubber and oil surging with the hiss of an air pump from the shop alongside. Before the blue front of the angular building, The Judge and another bent old man are perched on a wooden bench.

"Look out you don't drop that baby," The Judge calls out to Sister, waving his cane.

The sound of a human voice, somebody older who is watching over Sister, encourages her to slow, her breathing still fast and fear collecting in the top of her head where it steams under her sweaty hair.

When she gets to the café, she considers going in. Considers coming right out with everything—from petitions to threats—but figures that Marnie and Sade will either pass it off as nothing or start a big fuss. If everything comes out in the open, the town will have more reason than ever to put the children in foster homes.

One time Marnie went to a PTA meeting and cussed out all the teachers and other parents for "slurring" her good name—that's how she put it. The "cussing out" had stemmed from Sister and the twins going to school without lunch money. "Free lunches for poor children" had been the topic of discussion at the meeting that night, and

Janice Daugharty

Marnie had made it clear that she wouldn't put up with her children being treated like white trash. After that Sister and the boys were labeled not only poor but white trash for sure, and had to do without lunch.

In front of Sirman's station Sister begins to calm down. Ray Williams wouldn't dare come here. She believes that. But her calm vaporizes remembering that he had said he would have Lill and the twins put in foster homes if she failed to keep her end of the bargain. All she has gained by running home—which feels so good, so good!—is to have to crawl back. Lord in heaven help!

Passing into the cool stretch of shade before Miss Willington's house, she sees Willa and her three girls on the old lady's flower-pot-lined front porch. Miss Willington is bogged fat and satisfied in a straight chair while Willa winds her yellowish hair on permanent-wave rods. Larry the Cat, walking the picket fence, sits and curls his tail and eyes Sister. The girls, swinging on the left end of the porch, leap from the slat swing when they see her and straggle across the bare dirt yard toward the highway.

"Hey, Sister," Pat calls. "Where you been?"

Sister, on the other side of the highway, keeps walking, switching Lill to her other hip.

Willa stops winding Miss Willington's hair, watching Sister too. "Girls," she says low to Alda, Neida, and Pat, halting them. Just "Girls," meaning either "You can't play with Sister anymore," or "Don't bother Sister." Sister wonders which.

Later that evening, when Willa sends Alda and Neida to Sister's house with a pickle jug of milk, she knows.

"Mother said we could come play with you for a while," says Alda, eyeing the junk cars and woods as if picking out a place to play. Neida, pudgy in fresh yellow shorts and shirt, stands on the bottom doorstep and makes a game of hopping from the step to the ground, alternating flat bare feet.

"I can't play right now," says Sister and takes the milk from Alda, whose damp blond ringlets make her eyes look greener. She is wearing a green birthstone ring that matches her eyes, the same one Sister has been gambling for in the bubblegum machine at Sirman's.

They wait till Sister goes inside, then skip down the lane, sun striking their blond hair like sunflowers. Sister watches from her living room window. Willa, in her pink sundress, is standing on her porch, gazing up the lane, and after the two girls dash across the highway to the safety of their white house with mowed grass, flowers, and mother, all turn beautiful faces toward Sister's house, talking about ugly Sister.

All afternoon, since she got back from the fish camp, Sister has been battling the urge to go to Willa and tell on Ray Williams. But if Willa finds out about the problem with him, she may never let her girls play with Sister again. May think Sister knows too much now, for sure, and she does. And she feels years older than the girls who have skipped up the lane in the sunshine. Old and tired, but safe in the hot, trashy house where she will stay as long as she can to keep from facing Ray Williams again.

But when dusk comes and the church bell rings, endless steel gongs, Sister knows she will have to go back to Ray Williams to keep the twins and Lill from being sent off to foster homes.

Sister makes her next mistake by trying to scare the twins into behaving. She tells them about Ray Williams—not all of it, she can't bring herself to tell all of it, just the fact that he has said he will have them sent to foster homes if they don't quit ringing the church bell and breaking the courthouse windows. Until that night, when she sat them down in the kitchen and told what Ray Williams had said, she hadn't known for sure whether they had actually broken the windows.

They would show him, they said; they would fix that old man, might even bust out his car windows too. They would beat him up. While they rampage around the kitchen, foraging for food, she quarrels with them, threatening to go to the café and get Sade to come with his belt.

Go get him, they yell. We'll go get him ourselves. Like dogs in a pack, together they are brave.

Sister decides to change her tune, tells Mickey he

ought to be grateful to Ray Williams for going after him in Alabama. It sours her mouth to say such. And Mickey starts saying that Sade would have come after him anyway—*his daddy* would have come next Sunday. Sister makes another of numerous mistakes by spouting off that Sade is not Mickey's daddy and didn't give a damn if he never got home. At which point Mickey chases her around the kitchen with a butcher knife, slinging chairs from the table and trying to slash out her liver, and she hopes he does get sent to a foster home now, he and Paul and Lill, who is crying for her bottle.

~~~

Then Lill starts walking. Wobbly, testing steps, squealing and beaming and latching on to Sister's legs, more human and helpless than ever. Up to this point, she has seemed like a doll to be dressed and cuddled and put away. Now she toddles and falls and almost breaks. Bruised lumps standing on her porcelain forehead. She fusses, she frets, she clings, and only a sister could love her. Anybody else would have thrown her out and wished for a better doll next Christmas.

*S*ISTER CAN FEEL HERSELF
healing from the fish-camp episode, but each time she
remembers that she will have to go back, the wound opens
fresh.

She needs more time.

Just as she has overed wanting to play, she has overed
loving to surprise, and no longer feels the urge to tell
Marnie and Sade that Mickey is home. She doesn't care to
show off Lill's toddling, or tattle on the twins for fighting
and tearing up the house. She doesn't even feel the need
to inform Marnie and Sade that there is no more food left
in the kitchen, save milk from Willa's cow and a half
bottle of half-and-half, Sade's ulcer treatment. She knows
Mickey and Paul are eating something, somewhere; they
can't be snacking at Sirman's now that Sade is in debt to
him (Sister is wise to the creditor/debtor routine: mail,
visits, and finally the entire family being shunned by the
store owners they owe).

It has been a long, long time, to Sister's way of thinking, since she and the twins charged on Sade's account at Hoot Walters's store, and not all that long since Hoot gave up trying to collect. Just long enough, maybe.

Mr. King, whose new service station is set diagonally to Hoot's grocery at the corner crossing, is still mailing bills for cold drinks, candy, and gas bought before the Odums took their business to Hoot Walters, along with monthly statements of rent due—six months behind. And if he can catch Sister, he sends word to Sade that he is going to have him put in jail if he doesn't pay up.

After school let out last summer, Sister sort of "borrowed" Sueann Horton's clip-on roller skates and black patent Mary Janes. Skate key in her shorts pocket and feeling rich, but no socks and her heels were blistered before she had skated the sunny mile from the Sampson Camp to Troublesome Creek dip. Gliding down the dip and across both highways at once, right under the blinking red light and straight past the open door of King's angular, blue service station, she had stopped to rest and pee and explore the narrow restroom built onto the south side. No windows in the pool blue room, no sound; just the skate wheels slisking hollow on the tile squares as Sister sat on the toilet seat and peed—dumb, happy, and on hold. Blind coming in out of the sun, she had watched the room bloom from womb dark to first light. Her very own water adding to the water in the toilet, trickling like a spring in a cave. Whiffs of curing cement and glue and Sister's own copper smell. Rolled white paper on a spindle to her left that she could take home to her own dim, fetid outhouse, where she wipes on catalog paper. A couple of weeks before she had tried to thread her body through the hole in the wooden bench after spying a red-pied rat snake flowing across the doorframe.

Rested and relieved now, she pulled up her panties, flushed the toilet twice, inspecting the tank to see how it worked, then skated to the door, turned the knob, and yanked. And yanked. And yanked. The cool blue room turned into a tomb, punishment for the sort-of-borrowed skates. Panicky, hot, and off balance, she beat on the door till her hand bones ached. "Help! Help!" she yelled. "Let me out." No windows and no air and nobody to hear her. "Hey, somebody come let me out. Mr. King, help!" The echo of her private scared voice mocked her, a personal betrayal of brave Sister's fear. Entombed forever like Jesus but with stolen skates.

As she sat on the floor to pull off the skates and black patent shoes, the door swung wide, and there stood Mr. King, tall and godlike with a round face that looked molded of wet clay. "I been looking for one of Sade Odums's bunch to make a playhouse out of my closet," he said in that muffled voice. "Tell him I said to get on by here and pay up."

So the twins have to be begging from Hoot. Too many candy bars have passed through the door of the Odums's house for Mickey and Paul to be eating off the neighbors, most of whom long ago quit letting Sister and the twins take meals with them, either to force Marnie and Sade to take care of their own or to keep from fighting with Marnie, who has spread the word that her children are not charity cases, though not in those words exactly.

Sister is truly hungry now. She has used up her stash of Zero candy bars in the headboard alcoves of her bed, the bedroom suite too about to be repossessed by a furniture store in Valdosta. The blond chest and dresser and bed with gold chevron pulls that Marnie bought during one of her spending sprees and is now using as weapon and pay to get Sister to take care of the children for one whole year. If Sister doesn't clean the house, the suite goes back. If Sister complains, the suite goes back. If Sister doesn't quit running up charge accounts, the suite goes back.

Sister sets out up the lane, holding Lill's kitten-boned hand and letting her toddle alongside. She takes two step, trips, and Sister jerks her to her feet—fifteen minutes en route to the end of the short lane—and so far, Willa, who will scold Sister for jerking Lill's arm, hasn't shown on the sunny white porch.

Next to Ray Williams, Willa is the last person Sister wants to see this morning. Not only because she might be tempted to confess about Ray Williams messing with her, about the closed account at Sirman's station, about Mickey being gone but now home, about Sister herself being well on her way to becoming a whore like Marnie. Willa might make things worse by defending Sister—she hopes—and Willa is the one person in all of Cornerville who Sister has succeeded in getting to respect her. She hopes.

She lifts the baby by one arm and places her on her hip, hurrying the rest of the way up the lane to the highway, eyes down and scanning the gravel-laced dirt as she passes Sirman's station. She can feel the wiry old man watching from the door of his sign-plastered frame station where Sister has known the limits of pleasure and pain: Once while eating a Zero bar, she had stuck her finger in an empty, dangling light socket and tasted the white-hot surge of electricity shock the sugar in her mouth and spew from her nose as fumes. Like something scary she'd dreamed that no one else could see.

A white car is parked in front of the café, and as Sister walks around the rear bumper, she spies Lill's crushed bottle with glass spears still screwed to the nipple cap. Sister wonders if Lill sees it too, but if she does, she apparently doesn't recognize it, because she goes on gnawing her fingers with saliva streaming down her chest, which looks like someone has scribbled on it with ink. That's how sheer Lill is, and thin, so thin that her bowed belly looks like a snake's after swallowing a rabbit. Lill needs food, thinks Sister. And thinking that, Sister knows that Lill is her ticket to charging again at Hoot's store. She always hates it when people say, "What a cute baby!" because Lill is not at all cute. With her wispy white hair and barely blue eyes too large in her sharp face, she looks like a picture that didn't quite take. Just pitiful! Maybe Sister should have clamped the pink ribbon in the sprig of hair on her crown, but it makes her look like a gag gift. No point in trying to pretty Lill up. Sister hopes Hoot will take pity on the ghost of flesh in her arms and hand over some baby food, whether or not Sade has settled the Odums's debt.

Coming up on the courtyard, Sister picks out Ray Williams's blue car parked between two others, and seeing it brings back memories of it crawling along the cemetery road. She crosses 129 on impulse, keeping her eyes on the car all the way to the crossing. The windshield is spattered in a starburst.

"Lord in Heaven help!" she says, hobbling on the sides of her feet to keep from blistering her soles on the hot pavement. She figures Mickey and Paul did it and wonders what else, how far they will go, and is almost glad. A bright spot flares in her chest, signaling fear and elation, and enables her to pass through the open door of Hoot's store without passing out in a faint.

Sun blind, she tries to sort Hoot from the dusky shadows of cramped produce hampers and counters and shelves. He rises from behind the mahogany-trimmed glass candy counter, on her left, and nudges his half glasses higher on his nose. "You too, huh?" he mumbles, and tilts his head back, peering down at Sister with his top lip lifting his black mustache. Same color and hog-bristle texture as his wavy hair.

She stands Lill on the whittled-on counter between the bronze-embossed cash register and the candy case. "Mr. Hoot," she says. "I need to get a few groceries, if you can let me have 'em."

"How 'bout standing that baby down on the floor," he says and waves over the counter. No smile.

"She can just about walk," says Sister, standing her on the dusty planks and clutching her hand. "Looks like she's gone be bow-legged though, don't it?" Sister adds.

"Might oughta go over there to the Health Department." He leans over the counter with his great hands spread on top. "Get Miss Maggie to give you some cod-liver oil."

"I done have," lies Sister. "Miss Maggie says what she needs is to get off the bottle. Start her on baby food."

He tips his head back again and peeps down through his glasses at Sister. "I'd say so."

"Watch her walk." Sister squats, balancing Lill in the bothered square of sunlight from the front window, then backs and squats again and claps her hands. Lill squeals and toddles toward her, collapsing into Sister's arms like a windup troll with misshapen feet. The ugliest baby Sister has ever seen. She hugs her. "Ain't she cute, though?" says Sister.

Hoot shakes his head no. "But she'll come out of it, more'n likely." He plucks a cluster of green tickets from a nail next to the cash register and riffles through them. Now and then peeping over his half glasses.

Sister stands there swaying with Lill on her hip as if hearing a song in her head.

"What y'all call her?" he says.

"Lill. That's what I call her." Sister kisses the baby's sucked pale cheek. "Marnie says she looks like a Lily to her. That's how we come by the name."

"That so!" Hoot takes a lichen-green ledger from beneath the counter and, holding the bills in one hand, begins jotting figures with the other. Names printed in neat black ink at the top of each page, many Sister has seen on the Baptist church petition.

Suddenly he stops writing and tips his head so that Sister can see the brushes of black hair in his nostrils. "Go get what you have to have, Sister." Then he shakes his yellow pencil at her. "But not one thing more, you hear."

Now that she can get what she needs, she has to figure what she wants to get, and while she heads toward the four parallel shelves, backset from the platform of sunlight, she listens to Hoot grumbling about Sade's leftover debt, about his and Marnie's sorry ways.

"No candy," he yells. "I ain't letting y'all have no more candy on a credit, so don't ask."

"Yessir." She holds up a can of green beans to make it look good. "Beans okay?"

"Beans is okay." He goes on grumbling while Sister parades the aisles in search of something familiar, something she can cook; if not candy, something kin to candy. So far, she has a loaf of Sunbeam bread and a jar of peanut butter. Strawberry jam and cornflakes, a bag of sugar—each item carried separately to the counter to show her good intent and her burden—and the baby perched on her hip.

When she gets to the baby-food section, at the far end of the middle row, so dim she can barely see the print on the tiny jars, she picks out a couple of jars of carrots, which she doubts Lill will eat since she wouldn't eat them herself if she were starving, and some custard. She goes to the counter again and sets them on top, eyeing the open, propped boxes of Zero bars in the candy case.

"Go get that baby some beets to build her blood," Hoot says, thumping Lill's bird crest of white hair with his pencil. She grabs it. He takes it back, grunts.

Beets? thinks Sister. Punishment.

With a single jar of beets, she brings back a baby bottle and sets it on the counter.

"*Ba-ba!*" shrieks Lill, reaching for it.

"Not yet," says Sister to Lill.

"Thought you was weaning her off the bottle." Hoot pushes his glasses in place and eyes Sister squarely.

"I forgot," says Sister and starts to carry it back.

"*Ba-ba!*" cries Lill. And as Sister turns to leave it on the shelf, Lill begins crying in earnest. "*Ba-ba, ba-ba!*"

"Go on and get it," says Hoot. "Ten years from now, who's gone know the difference?"

~~~

Another week passes, and Sister's days are linked by alternate bouts of dreading school, still one month away, and dreading going to Ray Williams again. Sister has come to the conclusion that the new county commissioner might be just as afraid of her as she is of him. What if she should tell? What if she has already? But who would take her word? And what has he really done except swap the cost of gas to Alabama for her cleaning up the fish camp?

And with that line of thinking she is back where she started from. She will have to go to him again, if for no other reason than to find out if and when somebody—the sheriff or whoever—will be coming after Lill and the twins to take them away. She has to either keep or let go of that tension born of waiting for the next car slowing at the lane to be the sheriff or whoever.

She finds that what she doesn't know drives her crazier than what she does—a surprise about herself. Since the day she learned about pride and respect, and began thinking—not just feeling any more—she has believed that what she doesn't know is okay. Such as not going back to the café after learning that Marnie and Sade are selling more than hamburgers; not going to church so she can avoid knowing, and thus being caught up in, community proceedings to close the café. Which is still open. And if any other petitions have been tacked on the door, she hasn't heard. She hasn't been by to look; let Sade and Marnie get tarred and feathered for all she cares.

She hates Marnie.

When she and Sade finally discovered Mickey on the following Sunday after he got home, they claimed to have known he was there all along, didn't want to wake him when they came in after midnight. Five nights running? According to Sade, he had hired Ray Williams to go after Mickey. And though Sister thinks it is entirely possible that Sade had hired Ray Williams, she doesn't believe it. If she chooses to believe that, she will have to believe that Ray Williams is in cahoots with Marnie and Sade and is more crooked than she had thought, and she will start hoping that she and the twins and Lill are in less danger than she had thought. That Ray Williams might indeed be afraid that she will tell, and be believed, and not bother any of them again.

She doesn't want to hope only to have hope turn into shock. Like sticking her finger in the light socket at Sirman's station while eating a Zero bar.

On the last Saturday night in July, she finds that all of her hard thinking isn't worth spit.

—

Sister has started letting Lill sleep with her to keep from worrying all night that she'll be gone in the morning. Also to share the whiny fan, which, if she turns on herself alone, makes her feel more guilty than cool.

The yellowflies seem to have eaten all the mosquitoes, because the threatening whir of mosquitoes has been replaced by the sneaky silence of yellowflies. And then the maddening itch that leaves welts. She drifts off to sleep, trying to decide which is worse. Of course it's the yellowfly, because the yellowfly is the one now feeding on her flesh.

She opens her eyes to the same shade of darkness that was there when she'd closed them, listening beyond the whirring of the fan for a shout, a bang, a whisper. She has heard something, something has woke her. She frees Lill from the bogged center of the mattress and bunches her pillow under her own head, covering one ear.

This time she hears a voice, this time louder, this time distinctly calling her name. One of the twins—one of the twins is at her window, which is partially blocked by the headboard. She kneels at the head of the bed and peeps through the screened gap between the bed and the window, and spies two midgets in silhouette against the blackened woods. And suddenly she realizes—more shock—that she probably did see the baboon. That she hadn't only imagined his coconut face among the knotholes of the black gums. The baboon was actually this close to her!

"What are y'all into now?" she whispers.

"Sister, Sister," they hiss. Then one voice claims the other. "You ain't gone believe it." Then the other, like echoes. "Yeah, Sister, you gotta get up. Come do something."

That they don't get mad at her for accusing them scares her. Means whatever is up is about as bad as it can get. "What is it? Where?" she says.

"Down at the café . . . the café."

They are still. Too still. Two dark statues of child heroes. She wishes they would move, maybe quarrel. She tries to make them. To set everything back on normal course. "Y'all just trying to start something."

"Honest injun—"

"Swear to God—"

"We ain't."

"Y'all get on in the house," she says, without thinking: They always do the exact opposite of what they are told. She doesn't wait to see, simply hops off the bed. Since she has quit trying to be respectable, she doesn't have to get dressed; she is still wearing her red shirt and shorts from . . . Yesterday? Today? What time is it?

Sometimes her hair roots prickle when lightning or snakes are about to strike, and do so now. She starts to scoop Lill up but changes her mind. Whatever is going on at the café, she doesn't want Lill there. Sister feels almost relieved, even while panting with fear, because whatever it is doesn't involve somebody—the sheriff or whoever— taking Lill.

One time, while the whole Odums family was fighting, a six-foot diamondback rattler had wallowed from the woods to the front yard, and everybody had quit fighting to go out and kill the snake. Sade had hung it on a wooden post at the start of the lane, where it stayed till the buzzards pecked the jewels from its hide.

Yes, Sister is relieved. But when she gets to the end of the lane and sees furling flags of fire in front of the café, she forgets everything and everybody except Marnie. She runs along the shoulder of the road, past the two dark houses on the corner, praying with a tight belt of fear around her chest, but halts when she gets to Sirman's station and steps behind one of the gasoline tanks out front.

A gang of men in white robes and hoods are crisscrossing before the café entrance, hieing lit pine torches that feed fire and smoke into the murky air. A cloud of low churning smoke that seems to give life to the teeming night bugs.

"We done warned y'all our last," yells one through cupped hands.

"They in there," says another one. "Cut off the lights is what they done."

More mumbling and shuffling, like graveyard spooks. Pants legs show, and shoes—that's all—as if the rest of their bodies is ashamed.

"Maybe they slipped out the back and gone home." One of the men straggles from the shuffling group with the sheet sucking between his legs and traipses around the side nearest Sister toward the rear of the café.

Suddenly Sister is overcome with love for Marnie, with fear that Marnie will be burned alive, and it is all Sister's fault for hating her. For not going back to the café again, for not saving Marnie from herself—she can't help it. She can't help what she is. She's just Marnie being Marnie, and not all that bad when you get to know her: the Marnie who tells Sister secrets and takes her out riding in her blue

Ford Victoria. Marnie, who is so pretty when she's dressed up, that on one of those rides she got stopped by a cop for speeding and talked him out of giving her a ticket. What she has done—whoring and lying and who knows what else—she has done for Sister and the twins and Lill, to keep them in groceries and shoes and that blond bedroom suite, the only new furniture in the house. Sister's.

She starts to scream, but nothing comes out but a dry gurk. She tries to move, but her feet remain planted on the concrete platform as if they were set in the cement when it was poured. She can smell her own shame, something hot. Shame because she really can move, after all, and scream, but doesn't dare. She will go to her grave hating herself for wishing Marnie were like Willa, for choosing to save her own self to take care of Lill instead of saving Marnie.

The man who has gone around to the rear of the café strolls toward the front again. "They in there, I heard 'em talking."

Till then all the men have sounded the same. Like recorded voices built into their white hoods. Now Sister can pick out some of the voices she's heard before, but only one has a name.

"Let's call it off now," he says. Then yells toward the café, "But hear me in there, next time we gone take you out and whip you."

"Yeah," another calls out, peering through the front window. "Ain't gone put up with no more of this monkey business, right here in the churchyard."

Sister starts to turn around and go home, when she spies Mickey and Paul streaking from the rear of the café to the night woods behind the lot where katydids shriek.

"There went them boys again," says one of the men. "Up and down the road all hours."

Ray Williams's voice.

If Sister believes she can no longer be surprised, she's proven wrong on Sunday: Marnie and Sade are silent and shaky, talking in their room throughout the day. Sell the café? Did Sade say he might sell the café? Sister stays as close to their door as she can without getting caught eavesdropping, one of many things Marnie cannot abide. Maybe they will decide to move away from Cornerville, a real solution to the whole problem.

But in the vibrating whir of the fan, now in Sade and Marnie's room, she hears them discussing money. Can't afford to sell. Can't make the payments if we quit the numbers racket.

Numbers racket? Sister has to sit on the floor, she's so shook. What is the numbers racket? Does that mean that Marnie isn't whoring? Sister has to know. Whatever the numbers racket is, it seems almost respectable compared to whoring. But why the Ku Klux Klan? What is the numbers racket?

The only person she can ask who will know is Willa,

and Sister can't go over there on Sunday with Mr. Lamar home. She doesn't know why, doesn't have a reason except that he's a man and men are likely to pitch fits and generally don't want strange children and dogs hanging around their houses. And like gasoline fumes when a match is struck, men blow up. Sister has seen Mr. Lamar blow up at Willa and the girls, but still he seems tame compared to Sade, who throws chairs and socks Marnie when he is mad.

All day Sister listens to hear more from Sade and Marnie—will they leave Cornerville?—but they seem to backtrack over the same ground. Nothing new till Sade finally says, "Gambling ain't no more a sin than judging somebody." How he always justifies his drunken tirades and displaying snakes at the end of the lane.

"I tell you one thing," he says loud, then low, "I ain't gone be run off from my own place. I've worked my ass off to . . ." The fan absorbs the rest of it and half of Marnie's reply: "You! What about me?" Doubling back in their same tracks. Finally: "Okay," says Sade, "we just gotta lay low for a while."

Sister gets still. Does it matter whether gambling or whoring? The fact is that Ray Williams will be arranging for the children to be taken away regardless. She figures Marnie and Sade won't leave the café, even if she tells them the children are being threatened.

And then she realizes that the Klan visit might also have been meant as a warning to her from Ray Williams.

NOBODY IS GOING TO SAVE Sister. Nobody cares. Not the girls at the end of the lane, painting rainbows on the sky with a water hose sprayer. Not Willa, cleaning out the parakeet cage on the north end of her front porch.

Not The Judge, hobbling with his cane toward the courthouse.

Nor Mrs. Willington, stealing eggs from the hen nests hidden behind the wooden pillars under her house.

Not Mr. Sirman, pumping gas into the tank of a white car headed for Florida.

Not Marnie and Sade, "lying low" at the café with its clean windows now spiking light.

Not Lill, whose warm chest is pressed to Sister's chest.

Nor Hoot Walters, sweeping the slab of concrete where the Trailways bus comes and goes each Monday.

Not even the sheriff, whose office Sister passes on the way to Ray Williams's.

"I come to say I'm sorry I run off the other day at the cemetery."

Williams springs from his cradle-back chair with that smirky look on his tapered face that tells her she hasn't been wrong not to hope she'd been wrong in what she'd thought in the first place. That he would "do her" first chance he got. That redesigning the posters hadn't changed a thing. COUNTY COMMISSIONER painted in black letters on the open door is proof.

"Well, I be dogged!" he says and comes around and perches on the edge of his desk with his hands tucked in his armpits. "So you up to going back out there, huh?" He is speaking so low she can hardly hear him. She moves closer, 'cause she might as well. He won't kill her. She knows that. But knowing it doesn't make her heart quit hammering.

"I'm ready when you are." She doesn't blink.

"Can't you get nobody to take care of that baby?" He reaches out to touch Lill, and Sister switches her to her other hip.

"Nosir," she says.

He steps around Sister to the door and peeps out, then turns to her. Arms loose by his side and fingers fidgeting as if itching to touch. "Go on out yonder to the camp," he says. "Give me a little while, and I'll be on."

She goes out and along the dusty hall, hearing him whistling a tune she doesn't know.

~~~

When she gets to the crossing, south of the blinking red light, she sees Mickey and Paul coming out of Hoot's store with grape Popsicles and hangs her head as if she doesn't see them and crosses 129 to the rounded-off corner of asphalt before King's service station.

"Where you going?" yells Paul. He and Mickey scoot across 129, north of the intersection, facing her from the other side of 94. She doesn't answer. She walks west along the gravel shoulder of 94, so hot and scared and ashamed she thinks her face might pop.

Mr. King sees her and steps to the door, his bronze countenance and kingly stance proof of his privilege. "Tell Sade I'm fixing to sic the law on him if he don't show up with what's owing me."

Sister doesn't answer, keeps walking. Faster now, to keep Paul and Mickey from catching up. They do anyway. Staying to the right side of the highway, Sister on the left. Yelling across while two cars pass. A pulpwood truck. A milk truck. And yet nobody.

Facing the cemetery ramp, Sister darts across the highway, jogging Lill with her bottle. Just as Sister figured, the boys get bored when they fail to get her attention, and they wander off through the yard of graves and into the stand of gums and oaks on the riverbank. She almost cries, watching them vanish into the woods.

No. No getting around it this time. She has delayed paying what she owes long enough.

"Go," she whispers to the twins. "Go, I want you to go."

And Lill says, "Go." Her first true word.

Then Sister cries. Not loud and not hard, just deep till her tears blur the heat-white headstones of the cemetery, and then the cool green trees of the camp. The sound of her mewling blending with the water sheeting over the spillway.

Inside the screened shelter, which has lost its clean scent and now reeks of rancid lard, she sets Lill on the floor and pulls all the greasy pots and pans from the stove cabinet and piles them around Lill like a fort. Watching her grin and yank one and then the other to her. A terrible clatter striking the unhindered calm of crickets and waterspray.

When finally she hears Ray Williams's car motoring up the cemetery road and through the gate to the camp, she doesn't turn. She doesn't look. She doesn't turn, she doesn't look even as he gets out and snibs the car door shut, even as he opens the crying screen door, doesn't turn when he handles her shoulders, same as he did at church.

His oniony breath is on her right ear.

The baby licks the rim of a pot lid.

He touches Sister's right breast from behind. She sucks in. Frozen. So far only her teeth hurt. When she does turn—no, he turns her—smirky face old, but body slim as a boy's!—her feet scamper toward the door, her hands bump it open, and she is out. Running, running across the shadow-flocked dirt with rushing in her ears, either water from the spillway or her own blood.

She gets halfway to the pond before she realizes that she has left Lill, and decides to go back when she hears the car start, pot lids clank inside the shelter, and sees the blue car gliding toward her through the trees.

She starts to head around the west side of the pond, but glancing behind, sees the car swerve west, then east as she turns east. She might make it to the east section of woods if she hurries, but if she does, she will leave Lill. So she darts tree to tree, hearing the car door open and feet beating the dirt behind her.

She trots toward the spillway, where Troublesome Creek flows into the pond, and creeps onto the narrow concrete dam that appears molded of sheer tumbling water, end to end, and like Jesus walking on water, inches toward the other side that seems to stretch with every step, with every tug at her ankles and whorl under her feet that might at any moment sweep her into the sudsy brown pool below.

A fourth of the way across the dam, slipping through the water-combed grass, she looks back and sees Ray Williams standing at the other end, shucking off his shoes, his socks, rolling his pants legs till his white shins shine, and she edges on, almost pitching sidelong from the watery green felt of lichen. The rushing of water over the dam is deafening, but she thinks she hears Ray Williams laughing. Close, closer, closing in on her, though he's just stepped onto the dam. But he's coming, he's coming. And she's glad he's coming. If she can get to the midpoint of the dam, which she has marked by one belled cypress with serenely swaying moss that mocks the agitated water, she can make it to the other side and back to Lill. But she can't believe that he is creeping and laughing along the spillway, arms scarecrowed out for balance, instead of heading her off on the other side, and is heartened by the fact that he must be truly dumb, yet disheartened because his very belief that he can catch her on the dam might make it so.

She has to quit looking behind and simply keep moving ahead—she has made it beyond the midpoint, the stringy-barked cypress—and trust that he can't possibly negotiate the slippery surface of the concrete any quicker than she can. But her eyes keep drawing behind, and down, down to the bottomless pool beyond the slushing overflow that tries to fool her into believing that the foam is a cloud she could float away on. She wishes she could swim. She wishes that Sade had tossed her out to the deep black gar hole at Indian River, south of the bridge, same as he had done the twins when he took them all swimming last Fourth of July. Though then she had fought him like a mama cat, him drunk and slapping back and making light of the boys straggling from the black hole to the scalloped shallows and puking picnic wieners and water.

Suddenly the sound of laughter in the roll and thunder of water turns to shouts, thuds, and plunks. Sister stops and pivots with her arms flapping like crane wings and sees Ray Williams hunkering and dodging pine knots and roots, and Paul and Mickey poised on the bank behind like pitchers on a baseball mound. A raft of sticks and corky driftwood float from the foamy surf toward a warren of cypress knees where mother cypresses stand watch.

Williams lets out a final whoop and tumbles headlong into the pond, and with mixed feelings of salvation and doom, Sister eases toward the end of the dam, hearing only lids clacking and water slapping along the hassled mud of the shoreline.

PART 2

*H*EADING OUT OF THE screened shelter with Lill in her arms, Sister sees Ray Williams crawl to the east shore of the pond and sit. The boys are gone, as if they had never been. Part of her knows that Williams won't chase her down now, that it is over for now, but her body is set in running motion. So, as before, she runs along the cemetery fence, listening for his car, and then takes the path by the row of frame houses fronting the highway.

No second chances. Sister will have to go straight to Marnie and Sade and tell them they have to move away, that Lill and the twins are as good as gone if they don't. But when she gets to the café, she passes right by with her gaze leveled on the Lamar house shining white among the live-oak trunks.

Trotting along the wire fence of the side yard, toward the rear of the house, Sister can hear the measured churning and knocking of Willa's wringer-washer on the back porch. When she stops, facing Willa, who is feeding a blue towel through the wringer, her feet still feel as if they are running.

Willa looks down at Sister and lets the blue towel wind around the wringer rollers; they grind and chug like somebody choking. She jerks the black plug from a socket on the wall and the washer goes dead with a groan and the humming of locusts in the oaks fill the void.

"What in the world, Sister?" Willa eases from the half porch to the doorsteps with her arms out. "Hand me the baby," she says.

Sister shakes her head, gets a fresh hold on Lill. She is clammy and red-faced but placid.

"What happened?" Willa asks.

Sister tries to talk but only puffs of air come out. Her lips feel like they've been bee-stung.

Lill spies the fat yellow cat slinking along the concrete pillars under the porch where blue starchy water has backed from the washer drain ditch. She squeals. The cat hops to the doorsteps and curls its body around Willa's trim tan ankles. She lifts it away with the top of her foot, and it flows into the shadowy recesses under the house.

"I'm not trying to take the baby from you, Sister," says Willa. "Come sit here on the doorsteps. Let me get you some water."

Sister inches over to the plank steps and sits with Lill on her lap while Willa goes through the screen door to the kitchen, gets a glass of water and comes back and gives it to Sister. Willa's hand is damp and bleach scented. She sits beside Sister on the doorsteps, studying her face.

Larry the Cat comes again and flows like melted butter across the bottom step and caresses their calves. Lill reaches for him. The cat scoots.

"You can talk, Sister," says Willa. "Nobody's here but me. The girls are gone to play with Annie Law."

Sister drinks some water, then feeds some to Lill. Lill pokes her fist into the glass as Sister rests it on her own knee, festered sores of impetigo that match those on the baby's legs. Scrapes and scratches Sister hadn't noticed till now. Even her hands are briar clawed.

"Who bothered you?" says Willa.

Sister drinks again, feels water trickle down her chin to her chest. This time, when she tries to talk, words come between pants. "They fixing to take Lill and the twins."

Lill, hearing her name, gazes up, then fishes in the glass and sucks water from her fingers.

"Who is?" Willa leans toward Sister on the other end of the step for a better look at her face.

"Ray Williams."

"That what he said?"

Sister nods. "Said he was if I didn't clean up his fish camp."

"Clean his camp?"

And then the words froth like soap bubbles from Sister's mouth, telling and retelling till she gets it right. While Willa listens and mutters, mad, but not at Sister.

"Where are the twins now?" asks Willa.

Sister shrugs.

"Did you tell your mama?"

"Nope."

Lill wriggles free from Sister's arms, backs down the steps, and toddles to the starchy blue puddle. Plopping and paddling at the water.

"Listen, Sister," says Willa and slips her arm around Sister's shoulders, jostling her. "Now you listen good. Anytime a man or anybody starts stuff like that, you go to your mama and tell."

"She wouldn't listen—"

"It doesn't matter. Just go and let that person messing with you know you've gone. You hear?"

"Yes'm," says Sister. "But still Lill, Lill and the boys is fixing to be sent off."

"That might be the way of it; I won't lie. You're a big girl, and you know the facts. Looks like people have made up their minds. Wasn't just that rotten old Ray Williams's idea."

Sister starts to cry, low squeezing sobs that make Lill stop slapping water and peer up. "They can't have her," Sister says. "Can't have none of us."

"I think you probably won't be asked." Willa places her head next to Sister's; her bushy hair is stiff and smells of soap. Not the sweet kind, but clean.

"Honey, I can't promise you the children will be better off, but I can promise you they won't be any worse off. There are people out there who love little children, will give 'em a good home."

"But Lill's ugly—look at her."

"No she's not." Willa laughs, watching Lill crawl through the puddle, muddy from her toes to her nose. "She's just different. I think she's cute."

"You want her?"

"I can't take another baby to raise, but I know lots of people would want her."

"She ain't hardly no trouble."

"I know that; I've kept her."

"But I take care of her, I do." Sister stomps off the doorsteps and lifts Lill by one arm, her toes still dabbling in the puddle.

"Don't hold her like that, honey. Her arm's apt to pop out of the socket."

Sister sets the baby on her hip, looking at her stick arm with raw sores on it. "I don't generally do that." Sister is over crying, only snuffling. But just as her feet had kept running after she'd stopped, her crying keeps on inside. Like bleeding.

"Right now I think both of y'all could do with some dinner." Willa gets up, smoothing her yellow sundress with wide straps across her stocky shoulders. She must have a dozen sundresses in different colors, all cut from the same pattern.

"I ain't hungry," says Sister. "We done eat."

"Sister, listen." Willa steps to the dirt.

Sister stares off at the pecan orchard, south of the house—green trees and grass stippled with purple flowers—where the girls chase lightning bugs after supper.

"Look at me, Sister."

Sister looks at Willa.

"Do you want Lill to get sick, maybe die?"

"No'm, I don't."

"Well, she's got to have somebody to look after her right. She can't keep being dragged up and down the road, half fed. You see that cat there?"

Sister looks at the fat yellow cat nooning on a mound of clothes at the end of the porch.

"If I don't feed him, he can wander off and catch a rat. He can get by; Lill can't."

"What about me? She's got me."

Willa crosses her muscular brown arms. She has a vaccination scar on her upper right arm, a star just like Sister's.

"Well, she does," says Sister. "I do for her all the time."

"Sister, how long before one of the twins gets hit by a car or gets drowned in the river?"

"They ain't yet."

"No, and they might never. But if they did, if Lill took sick, how would you feel?"

Sister wanders off around the house in the air scented with bleach, starch, and stewing beef and can think of only one person who can have Lill. Now Sister has to make Willa want Lill.

—~—

Sister begins thinking of the twins as already gone. Better off in some place she can't picture. And once she has accepted that they will have to go, she is almost glad. Willa is right about them maybe getting hurt or worse. Sister can see that. What she has to do now—while she has time—is pretty Lill up so Willa will take her. If she has time she might even pick out somebody for the twins, though she can't imagine anyone she knows who doesn't know them by reputation or through personal experience. So placing them nearby is doubtful.

Sade and Marnie have cleaned up the café and started spending more time at the house, but Sister doesn't trust them. Even if all of Cornerville decide they have changed and agree to let them keep the children, there is always the problem with Ray Williams, who strangely enough, hardly seems like a problem anymore. Sister doesn't want to see him, steers clear of the courthouse, but isn't especially afraid of him, now that she has told Willa. But Sister knows he hasn't forgotten her, and now that the twins are in on it too, she figures he will step up his plans to get rid of them all, Marnie and Sade included.

School will begin in one week, and Sister will be there. She will leave Lill with Willa, same as last year, and Willa won't let anybody take her. She can trust Willa, and trusts Willa to fall in love with Lill.

Every morning till school starts, Sister dresses Lill in the short-waisted pink dress with lace on the collar, wraps a sprig of hair on her crown with pink ribbon, and sports her off to the house up the lane; then, in the evenings, she strips Lill down to her diaper, her bowed legs bruised and sore-crusted as a leper's.

When Lill is dolled up, her sores are barely noticeable to Sister, because attention is drawn to her ribbon and face and the dingy embroidered flowers on the smocked yoke. A bottle of milk or Kool-Aid—if Hoot will let Sister have it—always handy to keep her mouth shut. She looks cute without her rotting tooth shining; also she is quieter. Without the nipple in her mouth, she babbles "ba-ba" or "go." Her two words.

Late evenings, at home, Sister tries to teach her to say "Mama," a word Sister intends to use on Willa. She will work on "Daddy" for Mr. Lamar, but figures since he's hardly ever home, it hardly matters. Daddies in most households only work. It is the mothers who have the say-so over who lives in the houses; it is the mothers who should be named.

Sade and Marnie are still on their best behavior at the café but are showing signs of boredom at home. Since the KKK visit, they have been closing the café earlier, mostly fighting with the twins about ripped window screens and yellowflies and dogs raising fleas in the house, then sticking to their bedroom, where they hog the one electric fan and fight till they fall asleep.

When school starts, the first of September, Sister no longer bothers with dressing Lill up; by now Willa should have fallen in love with the baby if she is going to, Sister reasons. (Lill says "Mama" now, but usually looks right at Sister. Sister's working on that.) Besides, Sister no longer has time to dress Lill, and fleas have produced itchy red bumps on her chest, which Lill can't scratch with the tight-busted dress on.

At school Sister stays to herself, and during class often takes out the Baptist church petition and goes down the list of names trying to find somebody willing enough and Christian enough to take the twins. Somebody who doesn't know them by reputation or through personal experience. She locates a couple of prospects based on the fact that because she doesn't know them, they probably don't know the Odumses either. What Sister hopes to do, meanwhile, is keep the twins going to school till she gets them a home, then maybe everybody will have forgotten their summer pranks.

At some point Sade and Marnie have begun keeping the café open till midnight again, and Sister figures they are gambling again. She's watched them getting gradually braver and braver: the jukebox blaring during Wednesday-night prayer meetings, an increased number of cars and trucks parked along the front and sides of the café, Marnie in high heels and jeans and red lipstick. But so far the KKK has not paid them another visit, and the churches are silent, and Ray Williams might have drowned in the pond for all Sister knows.

She sees his car with the shattered windshield parked

in front of the courthouse. And then all four tires sitting flat on the blacktop, and she figures the twins have let the air out. Though she doesn't want to start anything about Ray Williams again, she does ask them if they let the air out, and they say no, they just salted the road to his camp with roofing tacks.

What Sister doesn't know is how much of the road has been salted till she stops by Hoot's store for bread after school and he tells her that a whole funeral procession, hearse included, got flat tires.

A mountain of flattened tires grows on the side of Mr. King's station in the late-evening sunhaze, where two Negro men jack cars and roll tires, the hiss of air pumps claiming the clicking of grasshoppers in the grass alley between Hoot's store and the post office.

Sister stands in the doorway of the store, next to Hoot, watching people throng around King's station, across the intersection.

"Ain't a soul in Cornerville been spared," says Hoot, leaning into the door jamb with his hands rolled in his white apron. "Who you reckon . . . ?" His hoot-owl eyes stretch as the long black hearse pulls out onto 94, nosing into the westward sun with its spanking black tires.

"I wouldn't of thought it," says Sister, torn between watching Hoot and watching the two Negro men working toward the end car in a line beyond the Masonic building. "I wouldn't of thought him being a county commissioner, he'd of done it."

"How's that?" Now Hoot is standing straight, so straight that Sister has to stare up as he peeps down through his half glasses.

"Said he was fixing to make it where people would stay out of his fish camp, what I hear." Sister sucks in, squeezing the loaf of lightbread in her arms.

"Huh-uh," says Hoot, locking his hands behind. "Don't make sense, not and him with flat tires too."

"Flat tires ain't nothing to Ray Williams, not if it'll keep people from finding out he's got a game going back there."

"A game?"

"Some kind of gambling."

"Numbers racket?"

"I don't know nothing about no numbers racket."

"But they do down at the café, I bet."

"You mean Sade and Marnie? Shoot! That ain't nothing but a front." Sister feels so strange spinning a web of Marnie talk from thin air that she has to lean against the other jamb to keep from floating off into the blue sky. "Ray Williams is the man."

"You know that for a fact?"

"Nosir. Not for a fact, just hear tell he is."

"Wellsir," says Hoot and lopes off across 129, toward the courthouse.

Sister starts home with her squashed bread.

A week later new posters go up for a new county commissioner to replace Ray Williams, whose name is mud, till regular election time next spring.

*S*ISTER'S BIRTHDAY IS SEPTEM-
ber 10, a time she associates with the mystery of still-hot
days while the sun lists southward, charting its fall course.
Sameness and change. A settling in for the tortuous days of
school: sleepy, itchy, pointless. Teachers in the same aired
and spot-cleaned dresses, and the girls Sister knows from
the year before transfigured into teenagers by pimples and
shaped hair. Boys gangly with sudden knots in their
throats that slide up and down when they duck-talk. And
Sister still the same faceless lump as last year, birthday or
not. Just one more day. One more day to get through, and
having gotten through it, feeling she's made it beyond that
expected point-of-turning, and can rest easy that she
hasn't changed.

Birthdays are secret. Shameful private days, because if
she had friends they might ask, "What did you get for your
birthday?" And if she doesn't lie, she'd have to say, I didn't
get anything, nobody remembered.

Not that Sister cares.

Already, she has watched Alda, Neida, and Pat have birthdays with the kitchen table dragged out in the front yard and cakes with pink and green candy words bogged in white icing. Presents in flower-sprigged paper with curly bows. Kool-Aid that turns their lips red. The confusion of other children around them while they stand out without even trying. Their names on everybody's lips. That expectation of change.

Sister likes this evenness of nobody knowing it's her birthday while inside bubbles, *It's my birthday!* A whole day at school, knowing and not telling, though it must show on her clear cheeky face, like pimples.

Her home room and history teacher, Miss Snow, new at Swanoochee County High, calls the roll with her withered hand flapping like a fish at her waist (somebody said polio, somebody else said the hand had worn out from using the paddle). Right off the bat she tries to scare the bad students into believing that smoking will kill them, and that the Negro students at the school across from the Sampson Camp will be moving to the white school. Nobody believes her. One of the good students, a girl, this time, takes the lunch report to the principal's office.

Sister likes the shuffling motion of changing classes because it helps keep her awake and makes the pointless days pass faster. In the seventh grade she would drift numb through whole days except when Miss Anner, her teacher then, would come down on her for not paying attention. Reminiscing now, Sister longs to pinch her hair between two fingers and feel the prickly ends on her thumb, like she used to, but she knows she'll never do that again at school. She tries not to think about it, and the clangy bell signaling class change helps ease the urge.

In a way she can understand why girls pair off to pass along the drab brown hall with its high ceilings—they don't stand out like Sister does by herself. But so far Sister hasn't come close to making a school friend. The boys with quacky voices shove around her, their long legs in tight jeans like pogo sticks.

She sees Alda going through a classroom door on the left side of the hall and is glad she doesn't have to test her friend-at-home. Would Alda speak at school, now that she's practically grown and popular? At school Sister has trouble picturing Alda and Neida at home in their cropped tops and shorts, or sometimes just their panties. At school they wear crisp cotton dresses with floating skirts and crinolines. Willa has handed some of them down to Sister, but she doesn't wear them to school: One, she fears Alda and Neida will hate her for showing everybody their last year's clothes; and two, the dresses are always dirty or lost in the heap of clothes that grows like garbage for Marnie to fuss about Sister not washing: If she doesn't wash them soon, Marnie will have the blond bedroom suite sent back to the Bakers Furniture Company, which mails regular threats to take it anyway because of payments past due.

At lunchtime you can tell the free-lunch kids from the pay-lunch kids by where they sit at the wall end of linked tables in the concrete-floored lunchroom. The free-lunch kids look dull and bow over their plates, and the pay-lunch kids lift bright faces and chat with one another. One thing they all have in common though is that all of them, pay-lunch kids and free, have pimples. Except Sister, whose skin is still smooth and bland and unmarked by bones. But it's her birthday—her secret birthday—and her face could change before the day is done.

She hates standing out as much as she hates lunch-room food—another secret, free lunches though Marnie has forbidden them—but doesn't expect to change because of the sameness of her status—just Sister!—and the same-ness of being grown since she can recall, or at least since Lill was born and passed along to Sister. Everybody else looks different since the seventh grade, as if the summer heat has expanded their bodies and warped their faces.

Today Sister finds herself remembering many of their birthdays in grade school when teachers used to make them stand for everybody to sing "Happy Birthday." She shivers, recalling how once she'd told and had to stand before the whole class while they yelled out the song, her secret. Nothing worse than having somebody who hates you sing to you. Though Sister feels fairly sure they don't hate her—they don't even know her—or like her.

During World History, her last class of the day, she has learned to watch for the sun to balance like a beach ball above the top frames of the west windows to signal when the bell will clang—school out for the day!

If she can get Lill to nap, after picking her up from Willa's, Sister might take a nap herself. But right now she is hungry; she wonders if she might talk Hoot into giving her one Zero bar on her way home. And an RC Cola, fizzy with the foamy malt in her mouth, sweet all the way down.

From the sidewalk, she can smell the burned diesel fumes of tandem buses filing past her, the sun already low behind the oaks touching branches over 94 all the way to the traffic light set to blink on red at the crossing.

She steps from the clear September sun into the hazy store with dust squiggles drifting, and can hear Hoot sliding and shuffling boxes behind the meat case at the rear.

Candy and gum, inside the mahogany case on her left, are highlighted by the sun through the front windows, a whole box of Zero candy bars, double stacked, in silvery green wrappings. All she has to do is step between the cash register counter and the front window and slip her hand into the glass case and snatch one Zero—maybe two—and be gone before he finds out she's been there. But as she starts around the cash register, she hears boxes stop sliding and looks up to see his swarthy questioning face above the white meat case.

Walking toward the front, between the center aisle of shelves, he rubs his black hair from his scowling forehead. "Thought I heard somebody," he says. "What can I do for you, Sister?"

"I just come by to tell you it's my birthday."

"Don't say." He wipes his hands on his bloody white bib apron and never takes his eyes off her as he sidles around and behind the cash register, then the candy counter. "You'd be what—thirteen, fourteen?"

"Fourteen." She can't believe she has told that it's her birthday. Her face burns.

"You know, they say this fourteen-year-old boy won hisself a hunderd-thousand dollars on some quiz show." One giant hand hovers over the open, tilted boxes of candy. "What'll it be, Sister?"

"A Zero?"

He picks up a bar and hands it over the counter. "Have a happy," he says and nods toward the door and strides out and around and up the center aisle of shelves toward the meat case.

She eats half of the bar while walking along the courtyard, birds twittering on the upper balcony of the white courthouse and breeze on her face, then wraps it up and pockets the rest. The gooey pull against her teeth makes her face ache. Before she gets to the café, strange in the fall slant of shadows from the oaks across the road, she changes sides where leaves rain down to the cooling gray dirt.

Now that she has let slip that it's her birthday, she might even tell her favorite person in the whole world, Willa. See what comes of it.

Alda, Neida, and Pat are already home and have changed into shorts and shirts. They are standing in the sideyard of the Lamar house, and when they spy Sister crossing their front yard to the porch, they duck behind the northwest corner of the house.

No, she won't tell. She fingers the candy bar in her skirt pocket, heading across the front porch, past Lill's empty playpen and through the door to the green living room.

Willa, in the kitchen, is standing with her back to Sister, whispering to the girls on the back porch through the screen door. Again, they eye Sister, then dart from view. Willa turns, walking toward Sister with her arms crossed over her white blouse.

Sister wonders if maybe they know it's her birthday and might be planning to surprise her. She cannot help looking at the long kitchen table for a cake. But there is only a cellophane pack of cookies and a bottle of cane syrup.

"Sister," says Willa.

Her not-smiling face makes Sister stop.

"Sister," she says again, "I've got some bad news for you."

"What?"

"Lill's gone."

"Gone where?" Sister knows without knowing that Marnie hasn't picked her up early. Happy Birthday.

"The welfare lady came and got her. I think she took her to that new teacher's house. Sandy Snow. Her sister lives with her and she's offered to take care of Lill while

Sandy's at school." Willa is reaching out as if to touch Sister, but draws her hand back to her blue plaid skirt.

Sister's fingers on the candy bar go numb.

"You know, they live in the big white house on Ninety-four, next to the schoolhouse, and . . .'"

"I know where they live at." Sister has just walked past there, not fifteen minutes ago. She leans in the kitchen doorway, scrubbing her back on the jamb. Her legs and arms and face itch too.

Pat steps into view again, still behind the back screened door, and starts crying, her small round face open and red, and Willa turns, eyeballing her. "I couldn't do a thing," Willa says, speaking to Sister again. "I tried. The welfare lady said—"

Sister butts in. "You could've kept Lill."

"No, I couldn't."

"You didn't want her."

"I did . . . I couldn't. I couldn't take another baby to raise."

"Wadn't nothing to it."

Willa tries to reach for Sister, who backs to the flat of the doorjamb and studies the graduating pencil marks where Willa has measured her girls' height on the opposite facing. As if to be sure their growth isn't a trick of the eye.

"Listen to me, Sister," says Willa, "listen. Like I said, I couldn't see taking another baby to raise, but I'll take you."

"Me?" Sister faces her.

Willa nods. "I talked to Wilmer and he said—"

"I'm not looking for no place to live."

"You have to."

"How come?"

"You're still a youngun in the law's eye."

"Me?"

Sister's confusion seems to confuse Willa. "I don't know why you'd think Lill and the twins would have to be put in homes and not you," Willa says.

"The twins—are they gone too?"

"I don't know; I expect so."

"They won't stay nowheres else."

"I heard they were fixing to be sent to Valdosta."

"Well, Marnie's gone have something to say about this."

"I expect she already has, her and Sade." Willa moves closer, and Sister steps into the cool green living room. "But The Judge has made up his mind."

"The Judge?" says Sister.

"This has been going on all summer, you know."

"Marnie and Sade don't know it, then. Wait till I tell 'em." Sister stands in the middle of the living room, with its sheer white crisscross curtains, where the southward arcing sun sheds its queer September light.

"They do know," says Willa, behind Sister at the front screen door. "I know for a fact your mama signed the papers."

Sister bursts through the door and jumps off the end of the porch, swinging the hanging parakeet cage and setting

Zelda to squawking, then trots along the path under the oaks. Mrs. Willington is rocking on her front porch with her head bowed. Sister doesn't even check for traffic, just runs on across 129 and through the door of the café.

Marnie stands with her arms crossed, peering out the front window on Sister's left, and slowly switches her fila-mented brown eyes when Sister pops through the door. "I kind of figured you'd be on back thisaway," Marnie says and drops her arms. She has on a yellow sleeveless shirt with stained breast pockets and blue jeans that show humps of fat on her thighs.

"They got Lill," says Sister. "I think they got the twins too."

"I know." Marnie walks toward the bar with her white sandals slapping on her leathern heels. "I'm the one got their stuff together."

"When?"

"A while ago."

"How come you to let 'em go?" Sister chokes back crying.

"Who am I up against a whole town?" Marnie waves both arms, then pulls a stool to the bar and sits, facing Sister on the other side. "You ever know me not to put up a fight for my younguns?"

"Couldn't you of just told 'em you was gone do better?"

"What you mean better?"

"Stay around the house more, look out for us."

"And how was I supposed to do that and work here at the same time?"

"Sade could've done it."

"Like shit!"

Suddenly Sister knows that Sade will be going too, if he hasn't gone already. The reason Marnie has been such a slob lately. The first sign. "You and Sade's busting up, right?"

"I never should've got hooked up with that loser in the first place."

"What about the café?"

"Sade's gone to see some man about taking it off his hands. Behind on the payments anyhow. Ready to roll on, he says."

"What about us?"

"I'm going to Jasper to live."

"Why didn't we do that before? Before—"

Marnie gets loud, looks loud. "Don't stand there and tell me what I ought and ought not of done."

"None of this wouldn't of happened if you'd picked up and moved to Jasper before—"

"When I want your two-cents' worth, I'll ask."

"You didn't care enough to even—"

Marnie leaps to her feet, reaches across the counter and slaps Sister's face. "Look at the pot calling the kettle black. You the one was s'posed to be keeping up with them. You the one got that blond bedroom suite for keeping them."

Sister steps away. "You gone try to get 'em back?"

Marnie props on the bar with her face buried in her puffy hands. "Ain't much point when I don't have no way of taking care of them. No money, nothing."

"We could go to the welfare."

"I got my pride."

"We done it before."

Marnie looks up with red-veined eyes. "Well, I ain't now."

"I could work. Me and you both."

"Doing what?"

"What you done before we come to Cornerville."

"*You* can't get a job waitressing." She swivels to the mirror, her eyes seeking Sister's around the gold-leaf flecking.

"We could both be whores."

"How'd you know about that?"

"I ain't blind."

"I had to do it. For y'all. Understand?"

"I don't care, if that's what you're thinking."

"I couldn't go through that again," Marnie says. "See, that's how come I couldn't keep y'all now. Not with me and Sade having our troubles."

Sister stands there, waiting for what she doesn't know.

"Look at me," says Marnie, not really speaking to Sister. "I'm a mess. I've let myself go. No man wouldn't look at me twice."

"You can fix up," says Sister. "I've seen you do it. You just need me to put you in a Toni. Maybe reduce."

"I ain't young no more."

"You ain't old neither."

"I feel old."

"Me too." Sister starts out.

"Sister," calls Marnie.

Sister stops, doesn't turn.

"You know I love you," says Marnie. "You know you've always been like a sister to me."

*S*ISTER WALKS HOME IN THE stretched shadows of oaks along 129, turning east down the lane toward the silent, no-color house where crickets sing in the background of gilt gum woods. It is cool now, so cool that the fine black hairs stand on her arms.

Lill's pink ribbon is laced in the dead leaves by the doorstep. Sister picks it up, wraps it around a finger till the tip is corded a curious bruise blue. Melon sunlight streaming through the west windows of the living room accents dust and bread crusts and bobby pins on the brown wood floor. She kicks aside one of her schoolbooks from last year. The one she couldn't find and has been dunned for every day since school started again. She can tell that the principal doesn't expect to get the book back and doesn't expect her to pay either. But it's all right now.

It's all right if she has to eat with the other free lunchers, if she has to beg at Hoot Walters's store; it's all right if Lill and the twins are gone—maybe they *are* better off. It's all right if the furniture company takes back the blond bedroom suite, which Sister stands contemplating in the eclipsing sunlight. But it's not all right if Marnie leaves Cornerville without Sister. She can't lie to herself and say that is all right.

She shucks the stained white sheets from her bed, grabs her bunched pillow, and slams it at the half-hidden window above the headboard. It lands on top of the hideaway shelf where she used to stash her Zero bars. Straining and grunting, she heaves the pee-steeped cotton mattress to the floor with one corner hiked on the box spring, tramps across it, and jerks at the left shelf door on the headboard till it snaps free and slings it behind, where it shatters the dresser mirror. Eyes on the mirror, she stomps across the box spring with its new-looking pink-striped ticking and snaps the other shelf door loose from the headboard and slings it at the mirror too, and this time splinters of glass clink to the dresser top, tipping over a bottle of Woodhue cologne Marnie had given to Sister to celebrate her period starting.

Now that her hands and feet are set in motion—now that she's dared to break the precious mirror of the precious blond dresser, she hops off the bed and snatches the drawers from the blond chest, hurling drawers and clothes to the slumped cotton mattress. When she's done, when drawers are toppled like a tower of ABC blocks, she scrunches in a corner of the dim room with the hand-me-down dresses from Willa and cries till her throat tightens. And stays, pinching her hair, till darkness covers the damaged blond bedroom suite.

And stays. And stays till she hears Sade come in, cursing as he knocks about the house, then leaving for what she knows is the last time. She knows how they—men—leave for the last time by the sound of their solid steps. A this-is-it sound; an I'm-leaving-and-by-God-I-won't-be-back sound in the gunning of the pickup up the lane. When Duke Hart, in Quitman, left Marnie, he backed over a neighbor child's red tricycle and dragged it up the street to the corner, depositing it on the curb like his broken heart.

She stays. And stays till Marnie comes in, plundering softly in the next room. Wire hangers on the broomstick rod, tacked wall to wall of one corner, slide and ding. Drawers open, close. Finally Marnie goes to the kitchen and shuts the back door, and still Sister doesn't breath easy till she hears Marnie go to her room again and spring the bed as she lies down.

Sunlight shedding through the east window over the headboard wakes Sister, and as always she listens to figure if some alarming sound has startled her awake. Nothing. Sister wonders if Marnie is still asleep, if she's gone. She gets up, tramping around the scattered clothes and the slumped mattress, spying herself in the shattered mirror that splinters her image: no eyes, black horns. A monster. The monster who has destroyed the precious blond bedroom suite used as pay for a job she didn't do.

Marnie is right. If Sister had taken good care of the twins and Lill, they would still be here.

"Marnie!" she calls, going out her bedroom door and into the next room, empty save for the same flowing sun and knots of clothes on the floor and bed. Not a piece of which, as Marnie would say, she would be caught dead in.

"Marnie?" Sister creeps through the room, smelling her mama, a stale deodorant scent mixed with Pond's face powder. A gap of empty hangers on the broomstick rod, drawers skewed from the old cherry bureau. A blue shirt of Sade's that Marnie used to wear to hide her hips when her weight was up.

If Marnie is gone, her car will be gone. But it has a flat tire. In the pink living room, Sister steps slow around the green couch, around Lill's crib, and through the open front door to the porch, gazing hollow-eyed at the empty spot where the blue-and-white car sat so long that the rain has etched out a car shape in the gray dirt.

Realizing that Marnie is gone now, Sister starts to cry, then feels a melancholy surge of relief because she doesn't have to dread Marnie getting mad and leaving her anymore. Marnie was always leaving, and now she is gone. Now Lill is gone. The twins are gone. Sister has nothing left to dread. Everybody is better off.

Except Sister.

~~~

But the feeling of relief won't hold.

She skips school the same day, because she can't imagine her aloneness not showing on her face, the face she still pictures minus eyes, plus horns. While eating the rest of her birthday Zero bar, overlooking the changing woods from the back doorsteps, she begins to believe that Marnie will come home again. If for no other reason than to get Sister to scratch her back where she can't reach. Who will polish Marnie's toenails when she gets overweight and can't bend? Who will sit up nights and listen to Marnie's problems with men till she finds a permanent one? Who will pluck caterpillars from Marnie's shirtsleeve and keep her from fainting?

Yes, she'll be back.

Sister tosses the candy wrapper into the yard with the rest of the trash—foil balls, brown and white paper, glass jars, and Spaghetti-O cans. A breeze off the gold woods picks up cool, and the crickets in the dog fennels and grass seem to be tiring down in keening clusters, worn out by the long hot summer.

How long can Sister stay by herself, she wonders, if Marnie doesn't come? She rambles about the house, checking for something, anything, that Marnie will have to come back for. She locates a new pair of black-and-white spectator pumps under the couch, and her heart lifts till she recalls how they had pinched Marnie's toes. That she'd rather go barefoot than be crippled. Marnie said.

Finally, when Sister can no longer bear pacing the

house or hiding out on the kitchen doorsteps to keep the neighbors from seeing her, she strikes out through the woods, where gophers have dredged white powdery sand from the dark loamy earth, behind Sirman's station and the café, scooting through yards across from the Baptist church and the courtyard, to the boxy white frame house near the school on 94 where Lill is supposed to be. She ducks behind a hedge of bushy plum trees, on the west side of the yard, and peeps through the yellowing leaves at the high-floored house. She can see one end of the screened porch and a chair rocking, the back of a woman's head, but can't make out who it is behind the gray mesh screen. She listens for Lill but hears only the chickering of blackbirds as they swoop in a net to the live oak behind the house. Acorns shower down in the storm of their wings.

When she hears the buses start and the shrieking of children set free from the schoolhouse, two lots east of Sandy Snow's house, she scurries along the yards and through the woods again, heading home.

She is hungry. Last night she'd thought she would never be hungry again, would never mind the dark again, but now she is hungry and eager for light to thwart the queer evening sun. For human voices. For Marnie and Lill (she doesn't miss the twins, a feeling that hurts more than missing Lill and Marnie).

She switches on all the lights—every light in the long house that is only two rooms wide. Three reasons for the lights: one, to displace the loneliness produced by the orange fall light, and two, to make Willa and the other neighbors believe that Marnie is still there. Three, to let Marnie know Sister is home waiting should she drive past.

Then Sister turns off all except the living room light. One reason: She can't afford to pay the electricity bill. She can't afford food. She can't afford rent. She can't afford water. The more she dwells on what she can't afford, the more panicky she becomes. So panicky that she paces the lit living room and presses her face to the night-blackened windows. Willa has left on her front porch light. Sister could go there. She could go and hear everybody talking and laughing and could even eat supper with them. She could watch Willa step and sway as she hands balls of pinched-off biscuit dough from her green bowl to her baked-brown pan. And then dab each flattened round with buttermilk. The oven giving off a warm, tangy smell while the girls deal plates to the table, and laugh, and trill forks and spoons—no knives, Sister doesn't have to bother with cutting up fried chicken.

Marnie will be back.

Finally, Sister, on the couch, worries herself to sleep, a cramped skimming sleep that thickens her tongue so that she couldn't scream for help if the monster in the mirror should pop through one of the paint-black windows. She watches the windows with her eyes closed, but the monster face doesn't show except on the undersides of her eyelids.

—

Next morning, she gets ready for school. She has to keep everybody believing that she's not alone, even though Marnie's Ford Victoria is gone, as well as Sade's white pickup. She has to hope the neighbors believe she's not alone. Especially Hoot and Willa and The Judge. Hoot, so that he will let her go on charging food—no more candy— and Willa, so that she won't tell the welfare lady that Marnie is already gone. The Judge, of course, is the real threat, the real Judas. Also, to get to school, Sister can walk right past her teacher's house, straight along the straight sidewalk, and legitimately spy on Lill.

She hopes that Sandy Snow's sister is rocking on the porch, rocking Lill, because Lill would like that. Or maybe Sandy's sister is having to rock Lill to stop her crying for Sister. Such thinking won't do, or Sister will start crying too and everybody will read on her monster face that her whole family has shattered like the mirror. That she is as alone as she deserves to be.

That old ready-to-pounce justifying melancholy creeps again, a feeling Sister prefers over guilt and fear, that feeling that will keep her from the kind of loneliness that will send her straight to the white house at the end of the lane where the porch light burns.

On her way to school, she sees Ray Williams getting out of his blue car in front of the courthouse, and she turns down the school bus shortcut, her usual route to school, and strolls past the one-cell brick jail on the south elbow of the courthouse square, then left at the brittle gray hotel with its swagged top gallery, to the sidewalk that will take her by her teacher's house. She walks slower, nearing the white frame house where, if she's lucky, she will see Lill. Her spirits droop as she gets to the screened front and sees no movement. Hears nothing. She keeps walking—maybe this afternoon, after school. One more chance today.

At school, she tries not to doze while Sandy Snow talks—an aging woman with a mocking girly voice—because if Sister doesn't keep up her schoolwork, this dumb new teacher might try to get in touch with Sister's parents. The old teachers know better. Also, Sister sits at attention to search for meaning in every snap of Sandy Snow's crow eyes, every flip of her withered hand. Once, she stops and stands so close to Sister that she can smell her coffee breath, and Sister expects her to mention Lill, maybe invite Sister to visit Lill, but she doesn't even say boo, just duck walks toward the blackboard and yanks the cord on the roll-up map of the world and it rotors wild and everybody laughs and the kidnapper says, "Now, class, that's uncalled-for."

Sister has written a note to the principal in her most careful cursive—"I'm so sorry about the lost book, but at last we have found it. Most Respectfully Yours, Marnie

Fiveash Odums"—and takes it to his office with the book. Though she loves "Most Respectfully Yours," which she has copied from a presidential letter in her history book, she feels it may not be right for Marnie. But one thing Sister has noticed: So far, if anybody knows Marnie is gone, nobody seems to care one way or the other. Except maybe Willa, with her porch light burning.

The pay-lunch kids who live in town always hike the sidewalk to and from school, and the free-lunch kids take the blacktop road, the shortcut used by buses transporting students to the south end of Swanoochee County. As if it's some kind of rule, this sidewalk segregation. Like Negroes not mixing with whites, Sister thinks. One more mystery. She has tried mixing with Negroes when Marnie moved into the quarters in Bainbridge. It hadn't worked. Not knowing that mixing Negroes with whites wouldn't work, Sister had attempted to chum with Sukey and Bugger, two tiny girls not much darker than Sister, and they had called her a Chink and chunked rocks at her.

Now Sister feels just as out of place, walking with the pay-lunch kids along the sidewalk, hanging back for them to walk ahead, so she can dally along the shallow grass strip of Sandy Snow's yard and spy on Lill.

Sueann Horton straggles from her giggling group to talk to Sister, and Sister gives her what Marnie would call the cold shoulder. No, Sister has not heard that Mary Nell Quick started (her period) and bled through on her white skirt; and no, she lied, she hasn't started her own period yet. Her face burns recalling having showed Sueann the tiny pricks in her nipples and being sent home by Sueann's mother for playing nasty.

Sueann in her polished brown penny loafers keeps step with Sister till they get to the magnolia with tarnished leaves on the corner of Sandy Snow's yard. Sister stops on the pretense of picking a sandspur from her sock, listening around Sueann's chatter about how she hates her mama and wonders if Sister hates hers too. Sister hears short quick footsteps inside the roomy old white house and wonders if they could be Lill's. Is she walking for real now? Sister can't see beyond the fly-wing-gray screen of the porch to tell whether the front door is open, but if she can continue gouging inside her sock for the nonexistent sandspur a little while longer, she might see Lill toddle out on the porch.

Then what? What if Lill sees Sister and starts crying for her?

Sister crosses the road, leaving Sueann staring after her, and paces up the adjacent sidewalk toward the intersection. Keeping step with Sueann, across 94, Sister gazes at the frame houses across from Sandy Snow's and then the Methodist church with the irresistible bell the twins used to ring. The post office, the pecan trees towering over the pitched blue roof—Sueann is still trotting to keep pace, watching Sister as if she knows she's been deserted—and Hoot's store.

Stepping in from the bright sun to the gloom of the

dusky store, Sister stands for her eyes to quit spangling orange.

"What can I do for you, Sister?" Hoot materializes from the center row of shelves.

"I guess some bread," she says. "A pack of Winstons for Marnie, too, if you can let me have them."

He stops at the end of the shelves, facing Sister. "You took up smoking?"

She freezes. "Nosir."

"Then you ain't gone need no smokes, are you?"

"I was just—"

"Go on and get what you gotta have," he says, "but don't play me for no fool."

"Yessir." Sister marches up the aisle of the nearest shelf. What will he do? Who will he tell? What if she puts off going to Willa's too long and ends up being sent to some strange place? She should go now. No, Marnie will be back.

"She's coming back," Sister calls.

"I ain't no social worker," he says.

"She just needed to get off to herself awhile."

He waits. "They's women like that."

Sister starts up the second row, grabbing a can of SpaghettiOs, and goes to the counter where Hoot waits. "She didn't just dump me, you know."

"I ain't said she did." He pushes his half-glasses up on his long thick nose, and his walled brown eyes magnify. "Sade gone yet?"

"Yessir, he took off." She places a loaf of bread and the SpaghettiOs on the counter.

"Reckon I oughta quit keeping a eye out for him to come pay, huh?"

She starts to pick up the groceries and put them on the shelves where they came from.

"I ain't cutting you off, Sister." He places his long-fingered hand on the bread. "Li'l ol' gal like you ain't got no business by herself. You get on over to Willa's first chance you get. Hear?"

"Marnie's coming back."

He snatches a brown paper sack from beneath the counter, slings it and pops it open. "Your ma can pick you up from over there."

Sister takes the sack of groceries and goes out. Choices. She can either stay home and hope the welfare lady doesn't show or go to Willa's; she can either cross to the courtyard and risk bumping into Ray Williams, or cross to Mr. King's side of the street and risk him dunning her for the rent. Since Ray Williams is nowhere in sight, but Mr. King is standing Godlike in the doorway of his station, she scoots along the courtyard railing with her head high.

When she gets to the café, she stops and stares through the plate-glass window, around the faded black "Sade's Café." A FOR SALE sign hangs on the door, and inside all is murky and still. Chairs on tops of tables with their legs up like the dead cockroach's. She goes on, walking faster past Mr. Sirman's station, and the two houses facing the Lamar house. No sign of The Judge on his porch. No sign of Willa or the girls, but Sister can hear them laughing and talking inside.

Hoot knows Sister is alone and maybe Sueann Horton and The Judge know; Willa and the girls suspect. Who else? Sister is so glad to be safe at home that she doesn't even mind being alone. Not much. She checks among the scattered clothes and trash to see if anything has been disturbed, if Marnie may have come while Sister was at school. Nothing she can detect is out of place, but it is hard to tell with so many clothes and so much trash, hard to take in all the order of the disorder and remember where what doesn't belong belongs.

Maybe she should clean up. Maybe if she does, Marnie will forgive her when she comes home. She starts with the living room, but soon finds that she's only shifting clothes and trash to the kitchen—she doesn't go into her bedroom, doesn't intend to, unless absolutely necessary. Then she cleans the kitchen, tossing soured dishrags and molded bread and cola bottles out the door where the low sun seems to hum with insects. When she gets through sweeping, the two rooms look neat but dusty in the hazy orange light slanting through the west windows. And she has learned that staying busy takes her mind off waiting for Marnie. Off Lill and the twins.

She heats the SpaghettiOs in a thin, dull pot, starts to leave the can on the stove but pitches it out the door. The sound of it clanging against the other cans stops the katydids' shrilling in the black gums. Sister gets still, feeling loneliness sweep over her. The katydids strike up singing again, and the sound seems to charge Sister's stalled heart.

While she is eating at the kitchen table, she hears a knock on the front doorsteps and eases up to peep around the open window over the porch. Alda and Neida are standing with a brown paper sack and a glass jug of milk.

"What y'all want?" Sister yells through the window.

"Mother sent you some milk and supper," says Alda, lifting her narrow face to the face in the window.

"I'm done eating," Sister says. "Marnie made spaghetti."

"Where's her car?"

"At Mr. King's. Being worked on."

"See if she'll let you come play this evening."

Sister steps back, mumbles into the air, pauses, steps to the window again and speaks up: "I gotta do homework, Marnie says."

They wait on the doorsteps for a few minutes. Then, "Mother said to tell you to come on over when you get ready," says Alda, watching Neida already walking up the lane.

"Tell her I'll stop by maybe in a couple of days."

Sister ducks aside to dismiss them and then peeps around to watch them disappear up the lane in the folding dusk.

They know.

*S*ISTER IS ALMOST AFRAID TO try the lights—how long does electricity stay on when the bill isn't paid?—but more afraid without them. Besides, she has to keep proving to the neighbors that Marnie and she still live here; she has to let Marnie know she is waiting.

Lights burn in the living room and kitchen, painting the panes of the windows black again, and like last night, Sister is afraid to look at the windows, afraid not to look.

Sitting on the ruptured green vinyl couch, doing her homework to prevent her teachers from trying to contact Marnie about her slack, she continues to glance up at the two west windows, divided by a dizzying pink wall, finally favoring the left window over the right window because it is nearer, easier to keep an eye on. Once she gets up and peers out and sees Willa's porch light shining up the lane. She really should go to Willa's, as Hoot told her to. No real reason not to go. Marnie's not coming.

But she might.

Sister sits again, cross-legged with her math book on her lap and a sheet of paper on the page opposite the one she's copying equations from. She has missed too many steps in this procedure to catch on now. Her eyes float free behind itchy lids; her head feels weighted, droops. Her neck stings. She rests her head on the back of the couch, closes her eyes, then sits up straight and listens to the hiss of dry leaves beyond the facing wall.

Again she watches the two empty windows, and like last night's image refreshed in her mind, pictures her monster face with no eyes and two horns projected on the black glass. The hissing sound stops, and she glances at the columns of math problems in the book on her lap. Eyes traveling up and darting from window to window, finally favoring the left over the right, and then to the right again, and Ray Williams's tapered face in dark glasses.

She drops the book on the floor and jumps up, hobbling to the front door with her left foot asleep to slip the latch on the facing into its matching brass slot. Then starts to the back door and stops in the kitchen, beholding Ray Williams.

"I wouldn't do no fancy screaming if I was you," he says and grins and steps toward her. "You just about done got on my bad side."

"What you want?" She hopes, even knowing better, that he'll say money for the gas to Alabama.

"It's just me and you now, Sister, ain't it?"

"Marnie's here."

"Marnie ain't studying you." He snorts, slings his head. "I been watching when you didn't know I was watching, and your mama's long gone."

Sister backs through the kitchen door to the living room with him keeping step, coming on, heavy on the screaky spots of rotting floor boards. He flips off the light switch in the kitchen when he gets to the doorway, his shadow falling long on the living room floor, on Sister.

If she runs toward the front, the motion might set him off and then it will be over—what will?—and make her heart beat too hard. She seems to be trying to keep her heart from beating her body to death. That's all.

"Where you want?" he says. "Here or in your room?" He nods toward her closed bedroom door.

"My room?"

"See, I'm giving you some say-so," he says, backing her, almost touching her with his short taut body. But not yet.

Just don't move quick, she says to herself; your heart will burst if you move quick. "I gotta go," she says.

He laughs. "Where?" And bumps her bedroom door open till it hits her dresser—*bap*!

"I don't know."

"Thought you was fixing to tell me you had to see bout that baby." He circles right to head her toward the bedroom door as she tries to sidle along the wall toward the front. She sidles back toward the kitchen, slowly, slowly, and he circles left and cuts her off. Faster, and her heart beats faster. To slow it, she slides along the wall toward her bedroom door again, but her heart has been set in motion anyway and is about to rupture from her chest like the springs in the green couch. So she turns quick and dashes into her bedroom and across the slumped mattress to the window half blocked by the headboard and breathes out what should be a scream.

On her knees now, on the box spring, holding to the precious blond headboard. Him yanking back on her left ankle and cackling. Face dragging over the new-looking pink-striped ticking to the stained slumped mattress on the floor. Her foot is ripping, her panties ripping, his right knee on her right hipbone and an elbow on her neck.

"Back or front?" he says, panting like a dog. "I'm giving you the say-so."

And then he does both. She doesn't know when he flipped her over, facing him, but she can see the two of them fused in the shattered mirror, a monster for real now.

~~~

From the slumped mattress Sister watches the block of electric light in the doorway melt into morning light; the same break in the wall that has carried Ray Williams away might bring him back. She has nothing to fear now except him, nothing to fear but his coming back.

While hitching up his skinny black pants, standing over her, he had promised to kill her if she told, because when her voice had finally found form, she'd warned him that she would tell Marnie—what Willa had told her to say. And he had laughed. Before the light in the doorway had started to melt, she'd believed that her body and mind were beyond ever having to function or feel again, but finds that her legs ache from the jacking of her knees, her wrenching around beneath him while he clutched her shoulders, her breasts. Her ribs hurt from his smothering pressure, and her neck is scrubbed raw from his beard. Between her legs is raw and wet, sticking the inner flesh of her thighs together. But the hot throb in her right ankle, where he had yanked her from the headboard, makes all other pain seem dull and distant.

When the sun comes, shining strong through the half-blocked window over her bed, and spikes in the broken mirror that multiplies images of the strange thick girl on the mattress, she gives into the drawing of her eyes and closes them. No more fear till the sun goes.

Waking up, she gasps and holds her breath, watching the block of light in the doorway for Ray Williams. Her room is dusky and dismal, and the sun has switched sides in the sky, filling the living room with light akin to last night's light.

She sits up, then edges off the mattress, staring at the puslike blood on the pink-striped ticking, then down at her bruised and blood-streaked legs, at her body that seems like somebody else's. She folds the mattress over onto the bed, bloody side down, hobbles out of the room, and closes the door. She will never again go into the room with the blond bedroom suite, which seems as much defiled by Ray Williams having peeped through her window when she wasn't aware as him raping her in the room when she was.

In the unceiled pantry, north of the kitchen, Sister washes with a white cloth left floating in a galvanized tin washtub of soap-filmed water. Maybe Marnie's bathwater. There is a spigot on the water-ringed west wall, with a black garden hose used for running water into and siphoning water from the tub; and on the south wall, dividing kitchen from pantry, a plank shelf anchored by slanted two-by-fours, on top of which sits a round white enamel pan with a red rim, and above it a square desilvering mirror with toothpaste spatters. The unpainted board floor is spongy and cool, smells of mold. Smells of stale water and damp clothes and the Odumses.

Sister goes into Marnie's room and pilfers through the pile of old clothes on the bed and finds a pair of navy blue slacks. She puts them on, walking on the hems to get to Sade's blue shirt by the door, the one Marnie used to wear when her weight was up.

While the sun across the kitchen floor switches shapes and shades, she makes a peanut-butter sandwich and sits at the square white table, watching the back door. Open because that's how Ray Williams has left it, and to close it means he might pop through again and make Sister's heart beat like bat wings in her chest. She has to make up her mind whether to go on to Willa's house or stay here in her own house that will soon brighten with the left-on living room light.

From where she sits she can see through the living room to the front door, the orangy sun growing denser in dusty squares on the brown wood floor. She keeps telling herself she should go now, she should go before dark, before . . . She should unstick herself from the chair and walk straight through the dusty light to the front door, slip the brass latch from its matching slot, and walk out and up the lane to the light that will be shining on the porch across the highway. She goes on saying I will go now, till the living room light begins to glow, at first dim and then bright, and then watches the block of grainy gray through the back door till the trees blend into the black sky.

And then she knows why she is stuck to the chair, why she is waiting, not trying to get away. Not for Marnie—she isn't waiting for her anymore—she is waiting for Ray Williams.

~~~

She gets up and goes to the dish drainer on the counter by the gummy white stove, takes the icepick and crosses the kitchen to the open back door and steps behind it. Scrunched sideways, she stands with her right hand raised, gripping the pick, till her right shoulder goes numb, then uses her left hand to support her right elbow. She can see the frame of light from the living room brighten as the dark thickens, then spill through the kitchen door, the frame of light like a movie screen where the picture will unfold: Sister in Marnie's slacks driving the icepick between Ray Williams's shoulder blades as he starts into the living room.

Just when she thinks she will go blind with watching, deaf with listening to the ringing of katydids and the cheeping of tree frogs, she hears the tinny clatter of cans against cans in the trash heap outside the back door. She catches her breath and holds it, feeling her skin prickle as if stuck to ice, while her insides feel drenched in boiling water. Then she hears a lapping sound, more clattering of cans, and sniffing. Faint tapping on the other side of the door. She freezes, watching for Ray Williams to show beyond the peep space of her hiding place, for him to step into the frame of light shedding from the living room.

A brown-and-tan hound sticks its rubbery black nose around the door, sniffs Sister. She kicks at the dog, and it yelps and scampers down the doorsteps. She can breathe, she can come out. Just a dog. Just a dog. She lowers the icepick, but still stands there, letting the blood drain down in her hand.

He won't come. Of course he won't come. He'd expect her to be gone after the nightmare of last night. Only a fool would stay. Only a fool would come back.

As she starts to step from behind the door, she hears leaves rustling outside the living room windows, then the kitchen, then the back door. In the trash pile, a bottle rolls and strikes another bottle, clink. She can feel somebody standing at the doorsteps, gazing into the kitchen, listening in rapt human fear or foolishness. Marnie? Sade looking for Marnie?

Then footsteps crunching in leaves again, past the door and along the rear wall of the house, stopping at Sister's bedroom window, and she knows it is Ray Williams. Hand raised, clutching the pick, fingers so numb she has to look at the pick to see if she is holding the handle, if the rusty metal point is up.

One more time around the house, and he is at the kitchen door again, on the steps, stopping, wondering, listening too.

And then Sister wishes she had gone to Willa's when she could go, with all her heart she wishes . . . She dreads the bat-wing beating of her heart when she will dash behind him in the frame of light, dreads how the pick will feel piercing bone and flesh. The sound of scuffling. What if she misses and he takes the icepick and rams it into her heart like the wooden stake driven into the devil's heart at the tent show she went to last summer?

He takes one more step, and she can see him through the crack in the back door, his thick hairy arm clearing the blind of her hiding place, and then his body, the side of his tapered face, the light glimmering on his tipped-up, green-tinted clip-on sunshades. The floor creaks, sending shivers up her spine.

She draws back, closing her eyes as if to keep him from seeing her, but opens them quickly, expecting to see him smirking at her. She can smell him, his raw oniony scent.

He moves toward the frame of light, floor creaking, with his side instead of his back to her. His slow shadow long across the floor. He has on a white shirt and black pants, black shoes, and white socks. When he turns, if he turns, she will do it. When he gets to the centerpoint of the lit block, she tips out with the icepick high, heart and lungs on hold, and for a second freezes, because he is in the doorway, out of the block of light on the kitchen floor where it should happen, peering toward her closed bedroom door.

She grips the icepick in both hands and lunges, not even aiming at the point between his shoulder blades, and as he turns, shock on his smooth tan face, she drives the pick into the hollow of his throat. Blood spurts to her own face. He hollers, clutching both her hands and wrenching the pick as if helping her, both of them sprawling and grappling on the living room floor.

As his grip relaxes, hands fluttering like birds on the shadow-scrambled floor, she rolls to her closed bedroom door, leaps up, and runs toward the front door. The latch is stuck and she has to pry it aside, while gazing back at Ray Williams in blood gloves.

She gets halfway up the lane, safe except for her

breathing in and not breathing out, and stops, facing the drawing porch light at the house across the highway. If she goes there now, with blood on her hands and face and clothes, what will happen? She'll have to tell them she has killed Ray Williams, then tell them why, and the embarrassment seems worse than the danger of being found out for murder.

But she can't go back to her own house; she can't bear seeing Ray Williams again, reliving the stabbing. All that blood. She can't stay where she is, and she can't go anywhere else. Marnie. She has to find Marnie. Marnie will fix this. Marnie will fix everything and take her to Jasper with her. Sister has to get to Jasper.

She stumbles to the end of the lane and heads south along the edge of The Judge's yard, to the road shoulder, her bare feet mincing in the gravel. The road ahead is lit only by starlight. Like gazing up through the leaky tin roof of her outhouse on a sunny day. She stops, hugging herself; she can't walk fifteen miles to Jasper. And the first car or truck that passes will see her bloody and panicky and pick her up and she'll be placed in a foster home for sure. Or jail.

The thought of jail—the one on the corner of the courthouse square where lonesome men call to people passing by—sends her scurrying back toward the lane.

She walks slowly home, eyes on the two lit windows of the living room, and knows he's in there, so strange and yet familiar. The fact that she has killed him makes her feel justified and rational. Calm almost. But when she gets to the house, she has to look through one of the living room windows to believe he is really there. Sprawled on the floor with his white shirt wicking blood. The hole in his throat now seeping blood like a spring. His glasses with the green-tinted clip-on shades, next to her bedroom door, seem more alien than Ray Williams's slack body.

What if he's not dead? What if he is? What if she gets inside—to do what she doesn't know—and he jumps up and grabs her? What if she gets sent to the electric chair?

She just stands there, watching through the window, to keep him from coming to life and sneaking up behind her, to be sure she's actually done what she seems to have done. Or to wake up if this is another nightmare. Her legs and arms are freezing, she needs to pee, she's thirsty. But if she takes her eyes from the blood mapping on the floor, he might not be there when she looks again, which will mean that he is behind her. She has to look behind; she has to. When she does, she seems to break the spell of believing that he can get up and get to her.

But still she cannot go inside.

She goes to the front doorsteps and sits with her back against the porch post and her eyes on the spreading red pool with the sprawled body, belly up.

*S*URE THAT RAY WILLIAMS IS
dead now, Sister watches the living room light melt into
daylight again, then watches Willa's porch light fade, and
Wilmer Lamar stride around the left side of the house to
his green pickup, get in, back out, and head south toward
his farm and turpentine woods near the Georgia/Florida
line. She watches a bread truck pass with its happy Sunbeam girl on the side, and the semis laboring north with
their mysterious burdens.

When Sister sees Alda, Neida, and Pat come out the
front door with their schoolbooks and vanish beyond the
corner house up the lane, and The Judge follow his cane-
pocked path downtown, when the morning settles in with
neighbor women hanging clothes on the lines and sweeping out the dirt brought in the day before, when Sister hears
the birds chirping wakeup calls in the trees, she trods up the
lane toward the sunny white house across the highway.

In the same manner in which she has seen Wilmer
Lamar and the girls go to the back to hose off before going

inside, Sister passes along the side of the house in a drift of bacon smoke and turns on the tall spigot bracketed to the old smokehouse and begins hosing cold water on her arms, her face, letting the bloody water trickle down Sade's blue shirt and Marnie's navy slacks.

Through the crystal blur of water and sun streaming around the house, she sees Willa standing on the porch next to her white barrel washer, holding up a pair of blue dungarees and staring at her. The wringer-washer is pulled out from the wall, with hillocks of sorted clothes around it on the floor.

"What's all that blood from, Sister?" Willa drops the dungarees to the white-clothes heap.

Sister starts to tell, then drinks from the spout of water till it tanks in her throat.

Willa is in the yard now, beside her now. Fresh in the pink sundress that makes her dark skin look darker. Her lips are pink. Her blue eyes teary.

"I had to kill that old man's been messing with me." Sister still holds the hose so that the arch of water is spattering mud onto the hem of Willa's pink dress.

"Ray Williams?"

"I had to." Sister turns off the spigot, staring at sunbursts of resin on the wide pine boards. "Night before last he busted in on me, so when he come back last night I killed him." She wipes her mouth with her arm, tastes blood like orange Popsicle. "Come in on me while I was doing my lessons and . . . what-you-call-it?"

"Good Lord amercy!" says Willa and begins wringing out the tail of Sade's shirt on Sister's body. Willa seems addled, mad, in the throes of a cleaning frenzy. "Let's get you on in the house and clean you up, then we'll go—"

"Huh-uh," says Sister, backing to the wall of the smokehouse. "I ain't fixing to go nowhere."

"Sister, don't," says Willa, following. "You're all upset."

"If you try and make me go somewhere, I'll just run away. I'm heading out to find Marnie soon as I get cleaned up."

"Listen to me, listen, Sister." Willa eases nearer, reaches out, and grabs hold of Sister's shoulders. "You gotta tell me where all this took place. Where the . . . where he's at."

Sister points toward the house up the lane, still in shadow.

"Over yonder, dead on the living room floor."

"Maybe he's not, honey. Maybe he's just bad hurt or—"

"He's dead. I been watching for him to come to all night long."

"Good Lord amercy!" Willa digs her fingers into her bushy brown hair and scratches furiously. "He *wouldn't* be dead."

"Come on," says Sister, starting around her. "I'll show you."

"Sister, listen," says Willa. "Why don't I just go get the sheriff and tell him what's happened."

"See that road yonder," says Sister, pointing again, this

time at the hazy southbound highway. "You do and I'm gone." Even saying it, she can't imagine it.

"But what else *can* we do?"

Sister loves hearing "we" instead of "you." "We gotta hide him or something."

"Oh, honey, you can't do that."

"I can." Sister hopes and prays Willa doesn't let her. Not by herself. She starts walking, listening for Willa behind. Hoping and praying too that Willa doesn't turn toward Cornerville when they get to the sun-streaked road, that she will follow Sister.

She does. Mum suddenly with her arms too stiff by her side. Sister slowing so that Willa is walking alongside, so that she doesn't end up being first to the house. The sun has struck over the woods and is warming the cool air, the blue nothingness of the September sky. When they get to the front doorsteps, Sister steps ahead onto the porch and stands back, peeking through the door with Willa at Ray Williams in his pool of blood. The wooden handle of the icepick driven into his throat looks like a peg to hang neckties on.

"Oh Lord!" Willa turns pale and steps to the end of the shady porch, overlooking the woods. "An icepick!"

Sister starts, "I had to—" still watching the body.

"Why didn't you just come tell me?" Willa seems mad again, this time at Sister. She glares at her with her tawny arms crossed.

"You mean after he raped me or before?"

"I don't know. I swannee to goodness, honey, I don't know."

Sister is glad to hear herself called "honey" again. "What we gone do now?"

"Sister," says Willa, pacing the porch, "you know as good as anybody, when you kill a man you have to answer to the law." She stops, facing Sister. "You do know that, don't you?"

Sister nods. "Generally."

"No 'generally' to it," says Willa. "And in a case like this, the law will likely take into account him raping you."

"You believe that bull?"

"I want to." Willa goes back to the door and leans and looks again. "I want to believe that rainbows are painted on the sky, one color at a time."

"But they ain't, are they?"

Willa shakes her head, waits, then, "Okay now," she says and goes to the doorsteps.

Sister is terrified that she is leaving, that she is saying, Okay now, it's your mess, clean it up—what she says sometimes to her girls when they mess up. But she is hurrying, with her head high, bringing order to disorder. Up the lane with Sister slisking behind in Marnie's wet slacks. Going after a shovel, a water hose, washing powder, and Clorox. Almost gay about gathering her cleaning tools. Willa doesn't know the law or even how to drive, but she can clean.

Once, her even white teeth clench when the back of

Ray Williams's head bumps down the back doorsteps, Sister tugging at one foot and Willa the other, but she just watches behind for whatever might trip her and keeps pulling at the body as if she's dragging out a mattress to sun. And when Sister stops on the edge of the woods, breathing hard, Willa motions her on deeper into the blackgums shedding their cured leaves like brown butterflies.

While blowflies blow Ray Williams's parted gray lips and his dingy walled eyes, Willa and Sister take turns spading the loamy black dirt, eyeing the body now and then to see if the grave measures long enough, deep enough, to cover his bloating gut.

They stop to rest, listening, but hear only locusts buzzing, voices piped from the quarters through the thick trees, leaves whispering down.

When Willa starts to dig again, a woodpecker pecks from his impossible sideways stance on a black-gum trunk, and she stops, leaning on the shovel handle, her rosy tan face inscrutable. "After all you been through," she says and starts digging again, quick spadesful, with relish.

Finally they roll Ray Williams into the grave and begin pitching and kicking dirt to cover him, walking down the dirt with their bare feet while looking up and off, but not at each other.

Then Sister follows Willa out of the woods in gusts of falling leaves, like scraps of brown paper sack covering their tracks and the raw dirt grave. And in like ritual of

Willa's spring cleaning, they hose down Sister's house, scrubbing with brooms and Clorox till the old boards shine, till the last smear of blood slips through the cracks to the unstirred dust below. While Sister is spraying down the walls and floor of her emptied bedroom, a rainbow fans across the watery light. She stops, exchanging looks with Willa in the doorway; then they start cleaning again.

In the backyard they pile trash, clothes, and mattresses and set them on fire, raking around the pyre of furling flames so that the woods don't catch. They watch till the fire burns to low seething coals, and then Sister goes inside and turns off the living room light.

So tired that her feet are dragging, Sister follows Willa up the lane and across the road to Willa's back porch, where they take off their muddy, bloody, soot-streaked clothes and tuck them beneath the piles on the porch floor, Sister's navy pants and blue shirt with the dark clothes, and Willa's sooty sundress in the light-clothes pile because it used to be pink.

And then they wash. They fill the washer tub, watching the clothes churn, then feed them through the wringers and hang them out to purify under the September moon.

That night, when the Lamar family gathers for supper, Willa is fresh and smiling as if she's rested all day. "Sister's gone be living with us from now on," she tells everybody. "Understand?"

~~~

Sister has missed two days of school—nothing new or even odd in her opinion—and next time she goes, she is carrying a note from Willa saying that Sister has been sick, and from now on Willa is in charge of her. With the note pressed into Sister's hand, Willa relays a message for Sister not to talk to anybody about Ray Williams: "Listen, don't talk. Understand?"

So Sister listens at school, at Hoot's store, at the post office, while Willa sews a rainbow array of dresses for the new member of the family on her treadle-foot Singer. Larry the Cat paws at the paddling treadle, as if helping. Willa is always fluttering like a hummingbird, and even when she sits on the porch each evening before supper, she's like a hummingbird hovering. Sister figures that her porch sitting is a duty, an offering to her husband and children and porch-sitting neighbors, what they expect. That Willa would like to be in motion, thoughtlessly darting from chore to chore. Sister and Willa eye each other, just as they eye the house at the east end of the lane. Have you heard anything yet? No, nothing.

*O*THER THAN LONE MOMENTS, usually at night, usually tucked tight in the blue-room bed with Alda or Neida, when Sister relives the vibration of the icepick on bone in her hand and shivers, she is simply relieved that Ray Williams is gone, that she doesn't have to be scared of him. Lonely as she is for Lill, and as much as she still listens and watches for her, going to and coming from school, Sister is glad to be safe. She has times of longing to be by herself, to be rid of Willa and her merry-go-round of housework. Sister has never been so neat, so miserably mannered, so safe.

She misses Marnie and the old times, riding in her car with the twins in the backseat, and has to remind herself that the old times were never as good as they seem. For instance: Going to see Nell, Marnie's mother in Macon. Beef-jerky thin with skin so swarthy she looked smoked. Even smelled smoked. Stringy rust hair with gray roots, and red ankle boots. She was mad when Marnie and the kids got there—kind of "pissed off," as she said, coming at a mad walk across 129, same highway that ran through Cor-

nerville with about a thousand more cars, all honking, all
"pissed off" too. "Blow your nose!" yelled Nell. "You'll get
more out of it." And then to her daughter and grandchildren, "Y'all come on in, if you can get in," and headed up
the sloped brick walk to the sloped little house that looked
like it might slide off the red clay wall to the intersecting
streets at any minute. A cardboard box of yellow baby
chicks on the half-walled front porch and a couple of dirt-
colored bunnies hopping from the rigged wooden porch
gate to the closed front door, dropping round pellets like
cotton stuffing with every hop. Magazines piled hip high in
the dim moldy living room, a dusty rose-and-green-print
couch, green chair, a parrot that squawked, "Nell hell!"
and two musty-smelling gerbils that rode round and round
on a treadmill, loading the air with squeaking. Ashtrays of
cigarette butts on every table.

It was Sunday in Macon, a spring morning with cherry
trees in bloom, and somewhere beyond the roar of crisscrossing traffic, church bells chimed, while Marnie, preg-
nant with Lill then, moped and griped about morning
sickness, and Nell tried to force-feed her what she called
"soda crackers," till finally they got around to arguing
about money and Marnie's brats, who had left open the
porch gate and let the bunnies go, and everybody wound
up chasing the hopping bunnies through the traffic till it
was time to go. Back along 129, heading south that
evening along the same highway Sister had believed that
morning would take them to some exotic city. Marnie and

Sister in the front seat, the twins in the back, and squashed bunnies at the end of the road.

~~

Sister has new shoes now, black ballerinas with grosgrain bows on the toes, but doesn't like wearing them because she can't keep from looking down while she walks and bumps into people and has to speak.

When the first dress, a glazy red cotton poplin, is set free from the Singer's needle, puckered at the seams, Sister is glad to hand over Alda's clothes she's been wearing. At first the girls treated her like spend-the-night company, but after weeks of spending nights and days and bathtimes with Sister, they begin to fuss with her like a sister.

"Y'all treat Sister like a sister," Willa has told them, and seemed to know that it wouldn't work, and that what she had just said didn't even sound right. "Understand?"

And so far Wilmer Lamar, stocky, blond, and tense, seems to accept, or at least tolerate, Sister as one more child in the house, or one more of Willa's charities. Though Sister suspects part of the discourse in the pink front room, next to the living room, involves quarreling over whether the household can afford Sister. She's already figured out that Wilmer Lamar, and not Willa, is responsible for letting Lill go to Sandy Snow's house. He doesn't like noise.

When he comes in to eat each evening—an event as businesslike and serious as his work—Willa shushes the girls or takes them out walking or sits on the porch with them. Sometimes, while the autumn light lasts and the weather is cool bordering on cold, she sends them out to play after supper, she and Wilmer watching from their porch rockers, and Sister finds that she no longer feels like playing. She has changed. Though her body is no longer bruised and sore, she can still feel the crush of Ray Williams that canceled her childhood like a mistake. So, she tries to sit on the porch with Willa and Wilmer, but can tell she stops them talking. The creak of rockers picking up where their voices have left off when she joins them. When he leaves them alone, going off to bed before good dark, Sister and Willa are left eyeing each other and the house up the lane dissolving into the approach of darkness from the east woods, where Ray Williams lies at what they hope is eternal rest—have you heard anything yet? No, nothing.

Then they hear something. At first only a mishmash of rumors: Ray Williams ran off with some woman; Ray Williams has been kidnapped; Ray Williams's car has been found at his fish camp and word is he's committed suicide, drowned in the pond or the river. *Didn't you know? Ray Williams was big into the numbers racket.* And finally, Poor Old Ray Williams has been murdered and a search party is organizing to hunt for his body.

Suddenly the whole town is looking for Ray Williams,

dutiful servant to Swanoochee County. And as long as word of mouth is only spit, Sister and Willa shrink but try to ignore the rumors. It will pass. But when the *Valdosta Herald* comes out with Ray Williams's disappearance as headlines, Willa and Sister begin taking shallow breaths and step up the housework.

Waiting supper for Wilmer Lamar that evening, Willa gathers the girls on the porch and sings while she rocks with Neida and Alda riding the chair arms, Pat on her lap, and Sister hovering over the back, nosing into Willa's leather-scented hair. While Willa sings in her whangy, nasal voice, "I'll Fly Away" and "In the Sweet By and By," they all watch the new family move into the house at the end of the lane.

Touched by fear of being found out, Sister stands on the rockers like water skis, and Willa stops rocking, still singing, and the burdened chair of breathing bodies goes tense. Wormlike blooms slow-rain from the live oaks and sail to the porch as the night breeze lifts, snagging on the white towel that shrouds the blue-green parakeet's cage.

The new family—the Harcourts, from Alabama or Tennessee—have come to work at Mr. King's sawmill on the east end of Swanoochee County. Two girls and a mama and a daddy, ideal looking from the distance, just as the Lamars had seemed ideal before Sister moved in with them. Now she knows that Larry the Cat covets the bird, that the Lamars argue, hurt, and get hungry and dirty just like everybody else. Just like Sister and Marnie and Lill and the twins used to do. Except that the current of their suffering and sassing is quickly channeled to laughter through the magical power of Willa and her sweet bossy ways.

Sister hopes the new girls are sissies. She hopes they are terrified of snakes and worms and frogs and never step past Sade's junk-car lot to the woods, which she hopes stay bedded with leaves that will hopefully rot solid over Ray Williams's ripening grave. She hopes the new neighbor's beagle pup, now sniffing around the darkening yard, doesn't ramble and dig. She hopes the blood inside the house, now being checked out by the new mama and daddy, doesn't surface like grease on the walls after scrubbing; that the girls, now snooping around the yard, like the blond bedroom suite better than Sister did.

And Sister can feel Willa, with the strong, hiked shoulders, thinking all that too, and maybe more, maybe wishing she'd have let Sister strike out for Florida to search for Marnie, whose face is beginning to blur in Sister's mind. Less than a month since Marnie has gone, and already her face is a blur.

The dog scamps toward the woods, along the path where Sister and Willa had drug the body, and Willa's singing cracks, her rocking stops, then she starts again, faster, rocker and song. Sister holds on to the chair back and grits her teeth.

So far the new girls look like sissies. So far they are sitting on the doorsteps where Sister used to sit with Lill, and the cool October evening settles into Sister's skull as the bright ache of homesickness.

Rushing out the door to school each morning, the Lamar girls find old socks and rags deposited in the yard by the new neighbors' dog. A hardened biscuit, like a chunk of concrete—reminder and unsolved mystery of Sister's sole baking attempt. And finally Ray Williams's dog-gnawed black plastic glasses with the green-tinted clip-on shades close by.

Every morning Willa polices the neat square yard, and when she happens on the glasses, she sucks in and sighs with relief and pockets them in her blue-striped skirt. One more undone now done. One more blessing bestowed along with the house and the milk cow and her precious girls. But what else have she and Sister overlooked at the crime spot? Hadn't they buried the glasses with the body?—neither can remember—and what if the body has been dug up too? Is The Judge accumulating other dog-gnawed evidence against them?

When they spy a white rag on the dewy grass of the side yard from the living room window, they hold their breath, hoping it isn't a scrap of Ray Williams's shirt. Each animal bone delivered to the Lamar yard could be human bone.

Early October, and the fish-camp pond is dragged for Ray Williams's body, and then the rising river along a two-mile stretch. He has simply vanished, and there is talk at school that he's been captured by men from Mars. A flying saucer has touched down in Cornerville.

Finally, on the first frosty day in October, Mrs. Ray decides to have a memorial service for him. No more searching. Time to lay the good politician to rest. The good politician is dead and done for, which beats the heck out of ruining his posthumous reputation by leaving room to rise the other embarrassing speculations.

School lets out for the occasion, and Willa makes up her mind to take the girls to the service. The weather is no longer changing. It is winter now, a chilled calm that burnishes the petals of Willa's pink zinnias. She cuts a bouquet for Sister to carry.

"It's over," Willa whispers to Sister and snips another worm-etched stem.

"Yeah," says Sister, holding the flowers. "Now if that old dog'll just get hit by a car."

At the funeral Sister sits on one of the middle pews on the left, next to Willa, and watches Mrs. Ray on the front pew to her right. Fat, gray, and dour in a navy nylon dress, she makes the Mr. Ray in Sister's mind seem young and spry. Mrs. Ray is surrounded by family and kin, and Sister identifies the odd couple's son by his dark wavy hair, dingy eye whites, and tapered head. Maybe twenty-five or thirty and neat in a black wool suit with his hands folded on his lap.

Throughout the service Sister is sure that the preacher and the politicians, delivering eulogies, either did not know Ray Williams or are lying: He was a kind man who loved children and often gave them candy and money and "never let his right hand know what his left hand was doing," they say. He served on the board of education, had been a county commissioner for the past few months (nobody mentions that he had just been ousted for salting the cemetery road with roofing tacks and being big man in the numbers racket).

The church pews are scantily packed—no people lined along the walls, outside and in, as Swanoochee Countians usually do at funerals. Sister wonders if so few people have come because there is no dead body to view. What she and Marnie used to do, then they'd talk about it for days.

A baby squeals out, two pews behind Sister, and she turns to see Lill stood like a stuffed bunny in an Easter basket on the lap of Sandy Snow's sister. Lill's hair is sprigged on top with a blue bow, and she is plump and smiling in a blue batiste dress with tiny mother-of-pearl buttons down the front. Setting eyes on Sister, she squeals again, and Sandy Snow's sister with a wart between her hard green eyes sets Lill on her lap. Next to her sits Sandy Snow with that lordly teacher look.

Suddenly Sister is slapped by the fact that her teacher—her teacher!—is half mama to Lill now, a fact that seems to reduce Sister's chances of ever getting Lill back.

Sandy Snow knows Sister personally, her bad habits and failings—marks against her like sins in God's book of life. And yet, at the same time, having made that connection buoys Sister's hopes. Sister can chum with the teacher—take out trash, carry reports to the office, comb her feathery brown hair while she suns at recess—and increase her chances of at least getting to play with Lill.

During the funeral Sister turns so many times and causes Lill to squeal that Willa has to nudge her to break the spell. And again Sister sits listening to the truth about Ray Williams that is a lie.

The fact that his body is not present makes it seem less of a funeral—none of the family even cries—and more of a church service, with Ray Williams now Jesus.

~~~

And then rest. Long Saturdays of watching the new wood-encased TV set in the green living room that has been dimmed to theater darkness by quilts hung over the windows to make the fuzzy images clearer on the small square screen. Loud, so that voices can be heard above the static—real live people laughing and talking and spiriting through the sandstorm that sometimes flips and rolls and reminds the four huddled girls that the real-life images aren't real. No talking, no standing—if you have to eat or go to the bathroom, you crawl out, dizzy and breath on hold, and crawl back—no listening to Willa knocking around the house and threatening to cut the cord that feeds the juice to the girls' make-believe world.

Until Willa announces she is going to drive.

Then they sit at attention, bleary-eyed, and follow her like zombies to the pickup left by Wilmer Lamar, who has gone to Valdosta with another man to haul his cows to the sale.

They sit close, dreamy-faced, in the cold October light that is intensified by the truck's webby window glass, and watch Willa finger the keys in the ignition, switch on and wait, breathing in and out and peering behind as she backs the pickup onto the highway, then change gears and judder south along 129 to the CITY LIMITS sign, at last gliding onto the sparkling ribbon of silver gravel that unravels around curves and streams between spool walls of green pines. Nobody talks, nobody stands, till Willa laughs, her full red mouth making up half her face, passionate and free and as dream spun as the women on TV.

"There's the farm, girls," she says, and they all kneel on the seat to watch the tall pines reel past on the bight of blue sky.

"That's nothing," says Alda, next to the window. "Let's go to Jasper."

"Not today," says Willa with her neck craned, already searching for a good wide ramp in the woods to turn the pickup around and go home before it changes into a pumpkin. There it is, this is it! But she overshoots the turnoff and has to back up and onto the sloped ramp, hits the clutch instead of the brakes and crashes into a brace of Wilmer Lamar's gum barrels. Foot on the brake, she goes pale and switches off the truck and gets out and goes to the rear, uprights the toppled barrels, and begins scooping the oozing gum with her hands and arms and dribbling it into the barrels.

Sister watches with the other girls for a few minutes, then gets out and begins scooping alongside Willa, gazing at her face—she can't take her eyes off Willa's troubled face—and inhaling the tart pine scent of rosin, now gluing her shirt to her chest. Willa is real, Willa hurts and hates like everybody else, which means that Sister's new clear magical world could go fuzzy as the TV screen at any time. Willa's rosin-glazed arms are flecked with thatch and pine bark; she is standing in a hardening honey pool with her brown shoes shellacked, and her eyes are fixed in an unfocused stare that doesn't even see Sister. What is she scared of? Who is she scared of? Why would a grown woman be scared?

Sister wants to tell her it's okay. To tell her not to be scared, we will fix this. If we buried a man together and cleaned up his blood, we can clean up this gum spill together, and who's to know? Together, forever, we can fix what's wrong and never be found out.

"Thank you, Sister," Willa says and smiles, and Sister knows it isn't fear that makes Willa scoop up the slow gum, but duty and reality—this is where our food and clothes come from. Doing what's necessary and not only what's safe.

Though Sister no longer plays with the Lamar girls, she works with them. This time for pay. Each with her own bucket, after school, they scavenge for nuts in the pecan grove, south of the house. When their croker bags get full, Willa will take them to Valdosta to sell the pecans at the market, and they will have money for the Halloween Carnival, coming up. Ten to fifteen cents a pound, depending. A lot of money if you can fill your bag with one hundred pounds. Problem is finding the brown-streaked, oblong nuts among the curled brown leaves in the cold-curled grass.

Your sack is lying slack on the ground. How many buckets to fill it? Stooping till you are bent when you try to stand, till your back and shoulders tingle and ache. Bucket half full after an hour out in the cold with your nose dripping. Your lips are chapped and dry, so you lick them. A lesson in chapped lips: Don't lick them. Don't lick, no matter how dry your lips feel.

After one week of after-school working, on Saturday, Sister decides to crawl, and when her knees are scraped and raw she empathizes with Lill, who had to crawl before she could walk.

When Sister and the girls go inside for lunch—bologna sandwiches and homemade potato chips, because Willa fears she's weaned Sister off junk food too fast—Willa tells Sister to knock off for the day. She needs her to run to the store for Sunday dinner fixings.

Sitting at the table with the other girls, Sister figures something new has been uncovered about Ray Williams, and that's why Willa is pulling her out of earshot of the other girls. Another of Willa's tricks, like having them pick up pecans to get them away from the TV set, like luring them into brushing their teeth by sticking foil stars on a chart by their names. Sister sits stiff, waiting, while the girls file out the back door with their buckets.

Washing dishes, Willa watches the girls through the side-set mullioned window over the yellow linoleum counter, then turns to Sister, drying her hands. "I don't know what good's gone come of this," she says, "and maybe it's not the right thing to do. But I've worked it out so you can go see Lill."

Sister presses her bologna sandwich between her palms, the way she used to do, to make the bread doughy. She nods, she can't speak; she is excited, terrified.

The kitchen smells bitter clean from the blue dish detergent in the dishpan, yet smoky from the hot grease in the black iron skillet on the stove.

"Let me tell you something first, okay?" Willa sits at the table, facing Sister, and begins raking bread crusts and potato chip crumbs and stacking plates while she talks. "Could be you'll get there and Lill won't remember you now, and that'll hurt. On the other hand, she might remember you and cry when you have to leave."

She gets up, carrying the stacked dishes to the counter. "I'd really like you to think about it before you go, before you do something that'll upset you both." While washing the heavy white plates, she looks back. "Right now I believe Lill's doing pretty good—maybe better than she ever has. She looks good—you saw that at the church house. And you aren't doing bad yourself."

"I still think about her."

"I know you do."

"I still miss her and the twins; I miss Marnie." Sister feels warm tears like blood build in her face. Now that she can go, she might not want to go. She'll feel shy, especially with her teacher—same as God—there. Suddenly she feels mad with Willa again for not keeping Lill.

Sister picks up her flattened sandwich and goes out the front, through the green living room with the dead TV set, to eat on the doorsteps.

Cold sun augers through the live-oak leaves, casting lacy patterns on the concrete walk. Two squirrels spiral up one of the oaks and begin barking; sounds like they are sucking air through their teeth. Sister feels confused, as if she doesn't know the way to Sandy Snow's house. What she will say when her teacher comes to the door seems more important than seeing Lill. Double confusion. She stares out at the sunny side patch of bony pecan trees and watches the girls skimming the grass for nuts and thinks of the job as fun by comparison. A carefree time before she knew she could go, and realizes that she no longer wants to take care of Lill. And then she cries. She places her head on her arms and flips the sandwich to the walk and sobs and sniffles till her face fills with blood, or tears, or both. She's been raped and she hasn't cried. She's killed a man and she hasn't cried; her own mama has dumped her and she has cried, but not for long. But now she is crying. Crying for a long time. Crying as if to make up for not crying. When she stops crying to cough, she hears Willa tipping through the living room to the kitchen, coughing too.

Sister gets up and walks down the doorsteps, across the yard and along the foot path under the oaks in front of Mrs. Willington's house. She knows she should have changed clothes—all those pretty dresses—but knows she may have changed her mind with her holey blue jeans. She has to see Lill happy and well and then let her go, or run away with her if she's sad and sick. Maybe hitchhike to Jasper, she and Lill, to find Marnie. But she doesn't want to. What she wants is to go back to Willa's house, back to school, thrilling in the excitement of the carnival coming up. That's how selfish she is. For all she knows the twins could be locked up in somebody's house, or in jail, in Valdosta. She should want them back, free and full of mischief. She doesn't want them back. But she still wants Marnie. She and Marnie by themselves: Marnie will take her if she's by herself. When Marnie comes—not *if*—they will be like they used to be. Like sisters.

At the front of the lofty white house, with its screened-in porch, cold under the waxy-leafed magnolia, she steps onto the concrete doorsteps and licks her chapped lips and wipes her nose on her brown-plaid flannel shirtsleeve.

Now that she has permission to see Lill, she can finally hear her squealing and padding along the hall inside. All those times Sister has passed and couldn't hear or see her, and now she can hear that Lill is happy and well. If she weren't happy and well would she be running and squealing that high-happy squeal?

Sister turns around and hikes up the sidewalk, letting her chapped lips dry.

*I*N THE COLD BREATH OF OCTO-
ber, on Halloween Eve, ghosts fashioned from bed sheets
twirl and sway from the naked branches of the black gums
behind Sister's old house. Carving jack-o'-lanterns with
the Lamar girls on their front porch, Sister cannot help
eyeing the haunted woods up the lane and wondering
how close the new family has come to discovering Ray
Williams's resting place.

Their beagle pup has quit dragging up remnants of Sister's past and now deposits only newspapers belonging to
The Judge and gnawed shoes belonging to everybody; no
two alike in size, color, or style. So Sister has quit worrying
about the dog unearthing Ray Williams. She has made it a
point to meet the new girls—real sissies, just as she'd
thought—and scare them with horror stories about a
baboon escaping from a circus to the woods behind their
house. So she's no longer worried about the girls either. It
is the young daddy always prowling the woods with his
.22 rifle that worries Sister. Though not much. The naked

gray limbs of the gum trees shine like iron against the blue sky.

Truth is, Sister's quit worrying about most things.

Like Willa, Sister has learned that staying busy staves off worry, same as guilt. When Sister's not working, she is playing now. Getting ready for the Halloween Carnival with pecan money in the pockets of her new blue jeans, sporting red plaid cuffs to match her flannel shirt.

The plasticlike skin of the pumpkin resists her knife, and she has to jab out the triangular eyes and nose of her jack-o'-lantern, the zigzag teeth, and the cap on top with its woody stem. She scoops the moist seeds and pulp to a newspaper spread on the porch and bogs her candle deep inside the cavern of the pumpkin, lights it with a match and sets her creation on the right baluster of the doorsteps, facing the other three girls' jack-o'-lanterns.

Experts at bringing plain pumpkins to life, they have finished first and have gone inside to get ready for the carnival.

Up the lane the new young daddy is burning leaves, and smoke braids from the flames and scuds south along the highway, where a car is slowing at the city limits sign.

Sister starts to go through the screen door, but stops when she recognizes the wallowing roar of Marnie's blue-and-white Ford Victoria. Marnie turns right, up the lane, not even glancing at the Lamar house, at Sister standing watch on the porch. At the end of the lane, Marnie stops and waits for the man minding the fire to stroll with his rake to the car window. He leans on the handle of the rake, talking to Marnie. In a few minutes Marnie circles the yard and heads the car down the lane and across the highway and parks between the two oaks in front the Lamar house.

She slides out, grinning, and struts up the walk with her fingers slid in the back pockets of her tight faded jeans. She has reduced to her favorite size, faint hipbones showing but keeping her butt.

"Well," she says to Sister, "ain't you even gone come give your best buddy a hug?"

Sister meets her at the doorsteps and hugs her, hands out to keep from staining Marnie's silky red shirt with pumpkin.

"How you been, Sister?" she says, with her red lips curling. She holds Sister away by the shoulders.

"Awright," says Sister, grinning too. She can smell Woodhue mixing with leaf smoke. "You looking good, Marnie."

Marnie drops Sister's shoulders and slaps her own thighs. "Been working on it, you know." She tousles Sister's hair. "Look at you! Growing like corn."

"Getting tall." Sister can't help cutting her eyes at the grinning jack-o'-lantern, which now seems childish. She is glad she got done with it before Marnie came. She can hear the girls squealing and splashing water in the finally completed bathroom, Willa prancing from stove to dishpan in the kitchen, where the smells of fried ham and baking biscuits announce supper.

"Bet you thought I wadn't coming back," says Marnie.

"I wondered," says Sister.

"I got me a little trailer out close to the movie theater where I'm working."

"What you do there?"

"A little of everything. Sell tickets, popcorn. Clean if Bailey says clean."

"Bailey?"

"Man owns the picture show. Sweet on me, so he don't ask much."

Sister nods.

"Pays good, I can say that." Marnie stares up the lane where smoke billows. "We're setting up housekeeping, so I thought I'd come see about getting that blond bedroom suite. You not using it, are you?"

Sister shakes her head. Wondering whether Baker Furniture finally made good on their threat to repossess. Does the new family like it so much they can't bear to part with it? Or hate it so much they hauled it off? Or maybe it just vanished like the rainbow Sister spied when she last saw the suite, or like the blood of Ray Williams when Willa's broom licked it with bleach.

"You wanta come in?" Sister says. "Willa's in the kitchen."

"Ain't got but a minute," says Marnie, "just dropped by." She turns, and Sister thinks she is leaving, but she plops on the concrete baluster next to Sister's jack-o'-lantern, sitting with her palms pressed between her knees.

"I ain't doing good atall, Sister," she says. "Not atall."

Sister goes to the porch post, standing above Marnie, and hugs it. She can feel the square corners and the magic of Halloween sapped.

Marnie stares up at her with a wrung face, liver-pied patches that her makeup can't hide. "Got to where I can't hardly stand being by myself."

"What about Bailey?"

Marnie crosses her arms. "Married. Got a wife and a bunch of younguns. You know how it goes."

"Yeah," says Sister, holding her breath.

"What I figgered was, maybe you'd like to come go with me to Jasper, now I've got a li'l ol' place of my own."

Sister can feel Willa standing behind the screened door before she speaks. "How you, Marnie?" she says.

"Awright," says Marnie. "How 'bout you, Willa?"

"Doing fine," says Willa. "We're all doing fine."

"Me and Sister was just catching up on old times, so to speak."

"Well, Sister's gonna miss her Halloween if she doesn't come on and eat and get going."

Marnie gazes up at Sister. "Don't think I don't 'preciate all you done, Willa, but I think Sister's gone go on to Jasper with me. I been missing my little buddy." She winks at Sister.

"Sister's missed you too," says Willa in a tone that says more than the words.

"Well," says Marnie, standing. "What you say, Sister?"

Sister looks back at Willa but gets no signal. "I can't go just yet, Marnie," says Sister. "I been helping Willa and them out."

"When you reckon, then?" says Marnie.

"When?"

"Yeah, I could come back by in a week or so."

"That'd be good," says Sister. "In a week or so, we oughta be done picking up pecans."

"Well, I'll see you then," says Marnie, sliding her fingers in her hip pockets again. "They got *some* fire going over there, ain't they?" She stops at her car, staring over the white top at the bonfire, where ghosts dip on the backdrop of wintering woods.

"Go if you want to, Sister," says Willa. "I don't want to hold you back."

"I don't," says Sister, watching Marnie get into the car, check her lipstick in the rearview mirror, and motor south through the soft smoke. "I don't think she cares where I do or don't," says Sister. "Do you?"

"I don't know about her," says Willa, "but I care."

"You want me to stay?"

"I do," Willa says. "The girls do."

And already Sister's old longing to be with Marnie is only soreness following an ache.